Island Hope

Wildflower B&B Romance Series
Island Refuge
Island Dreams
Island Christmas
Island Hope

Island Hope

Wildflower B&B Romance 4

by
Kimberly Rose Johnson

ISLAND HOPE
Published by Mountain Brook Ink
White Salmon, WA U.S.A.

The website addresses shown in this book are not intended in any way to be or imply an endorsement on the part of Mountain Brook Ink, nor do we vouch for their content.

This story is a work of fiction. All characters and events are the product of the author's imagination. Any resemblance to any person, living or dead, is coincidental.

Scripture quotations are taken from the New King James Version of the Bible. Public domain.
ISBN: 978-1-943959-006

The Team: Miralee Ferrell, Nikki Wright, Cindy Jackson, Kathy Davis.
Cover: Indie Cover Design, Lynnette Bonner Designer.

Mountain Brook Ink is an inspirational publisher offering fiction you can believe in.

Printed in the United States of America

ACKNOWLEDGMENTS

It has been so much fun writing this series. It's bittersweet to say goodbye to the cast of Wildflower B&B Romance series. But as they say, all good things come to an end. I look forward to writing a new series, Sunriver Dreams, which takes place in one of my favorite places, Sunriver, Oregon.

Special thanks to everyone who had a hand in making this book what it is. You know who you are, and I appreciate each and every one of you. Thank you!

DEDICATION

To Shirley Blanchard. Thanks for the idea to include Easter into this story and for being such an encouragement to me. I appreciate you, my friend.

CHAPTER ONE

Derrick Trainor sat in Piper Grayson's office at the Wildflower Resort Lodge. The view from the window wasn't great considering that Piper owned the place, but who could complain about sunshine and blue sky, even if she could only see the parking lot? His attention shifted to his boss who sat behind her sleek, glass topped desk, her face twisted with worry. Unease settled on his shoulders.

"I appreciate all you've done at the resort, Derrick, but I need to make some changes."

His stomach churned. Was he about to get fired? "I've enjoyed working here. What's changing?"

"As you know, I'm six months pregnant, but what you don't know is that I've been put on bed rest. Effective immediately you will be the acting manager of Wildflower Resort and Spa. I know we talked about you taking over while I'm on maternity leave, and that you were concerned about the long hours during that time. I hope you can make this work because I'd hate to bring in someone new."

His pulse thrummed in his ears. "No, it's fine. Are you and the baby okay?" He'd begun to make changes at home to accommodate the longer hours he would be working in a few months, but he wasn't there yet. How would his fifteen-year-old daughter, Alyssa, handle him working sixty-hour weeks?

"My baby and I are okay, but my blood pressure is too high—has been for a while now."

No wonder Piper's health was at risk. She had too much on her plate. Between dealing with the fire and water damage that ruined twenty rooms at the north end of the building, and the construction of the cabins for phase two of the resort, anyone would have high blood pressure.

She continued. "I know you will do an exemplary job in my absence."

He nodded. Talk about a switch. A minute ago he'd thought he was about to be fired.

"Knock. Knock."

He turned toward the door and spotted a raven-haired woman with pale skin and classical facial features. She was stunning even in a hoodie, ripped jeans, and work boots, which he didn't find so attractive. She'd turn heads if she made an effort. Maybe she worked in the gardens with Chase, Piper's husband.

"Hope." Piper smiled and stood, though a little slower than usual. "I'd like you to meet Derrick Trainor. He'll be acting as manager until I return. You will need to run your schedule by him before you start any work, and he'll check over all work done each day."

Hope frowned. "Okay."

Derrick shook his head. "I'm sorry, but I'm not following."

"Close the door and have a seat, Hope."

The woman sat beside him. "Hope Michaels." She offered her hand. Deep purple nail polish covered her neatly trimmed nails.

"It's nice to meet you." He shook her hand then turned to Piper. That unsettled feeling resurfaced.

"Hope is the owner of the electrical company I hired to re-wire the section of the building that caught fire last month. Her company will also be doing all the electrical work on the cabins."

Hope removed her hoodie revealing arms with several tattoos. He didn't care for body art, but to each his own, or in this case, her own.

"Derrick, because of your background in electrical work, I thought it would be fitting for you to oversee this aspect of the project." Her attention shifted to Hope. "Having a second set of eyes is no reflection on your quality of work, Hope. But after the fire I'd feel more comfortable if Derrick double-checked everything. Chase will be dealing with the rest of the subcontractors and coordinating the timelines."

Hope's face reddened. Clearly she wasn't happy with Piper's arrangement. He was an electrician by trade but hadn't enjoyed it. After doing odd jobs he fell into his position here as assistant manager. He looked from his boss to Hope. The tension in the room was so thick it'd take a chainsaw to cut through.

"Thanks for stopping in, Hope."

The woman stood, but to her credit she didn't argue with Piper, though he suspected she had a few choice words for his boss. "Take care of yourself, Piper." She grabbed her hoodie and strode from the room leaving the door open behind her.

He turned to Piper. "That was awkward."

She wore a mischievous grin. "You've heard the phrase don't judge a book by its cover?"

He nodded.

"It applies to Hope. She's a friend, and in spite of what I said, I don't expect there to be any issues."

"Then why am I inspecting her work? You realize an actual inspector will do that?"

She gave him a look that clearly said he was trying her patience. Time to keep his thoughts to himself. But what exactly was Piper hinting at when she said not to judge a book—or Hope—by her cover? Sure she looked a little rough around the edges, but if his boss had confidence in her abilities, so did he.

Although he hadn't been working in the electrical field for several years, he kept up to date on everything. He didn't want to close the door on what he'd spent so much time and money learning to do.

"Hunt Enterprises, my father's development company, has used Hope's company on multiple projects. She does excellent work. I only wish she'd been available to do the job here when we were building. We probably wouldn't have had that electrical fire last month."

This was high praise coming from his boss—but even given her paranoia something didn't add up. Piper was fair and called things how she saw them whether good or bad, so what was he missing?

Piper continued to talk, and he focused on her words again. "I've arranged for her to stay at Wildflower B&B since we are booked for the summer."

His sister managed the B&B. He almost laughed. Jill was as straight-laced as a person could get. Her eyes had probably bugged out when she saw the art on Hope's arms.

He tabled the thought for now. He had enough to worry about with the new responsibilities given to him today. "Sounds good. I assume you want me to update you on what's going on in the day-to-day operations."

She shook her head. "As much as I want that, my doctor suggested I allow Chase to filter what information I receive."

Whoa. This must be serious. Piper was hands-on. It must be killing her to release control. Besides that, Chase not only took care of the grounds at the resort, he had a flourishing landscape and design business that often took him away from the island.

"Any questions?"

"Not right now. If I come up with any may I call you?"

She shook her head. "Talk to Chase. He'll stop in every morning and then again in the evenings. If something urgent arises call Chase's cell phone."

Derrick nodded. Things were about to get very interesting.

Hope stormed through the lobby and out the automatic sliding glass doors. The nerve! She was a Master Electrician and highly respected in her industry. Why would Piper want a dude with a vague background in electrical work to supervise her? There was nothing worse than a person who knew a little about something and tried to act like they were experts. He would probably get in her way and cause problems. The whole thing was insulting!

Her phone rang, and she pulled it from her back pocket. "Hope speaking."

"It's Piper. I think I owe you an explanation."

"You don't owe me anything." The last thing she wanted to do was upset her friend, so she'd keep her thoughts to herself, unless that Derrick guy became a problem.

"You and I have been friends for years, and I've known Derrick for three years. He's a good man, but he's lonely. I think the two of you would hit it off."

Hope stopped moving. A car beeped its horn. She waved and moved out of the way. "Come again? Are you seriously trying to set me up?"

"Well . . ."

"I quit." Her crew wouldn't be happy, but she was sure they'd appreciate not having to commute via ferry from the mainland every day. Being single with no children, she preferred to stay close to the project.

"No! Please, Hope. I need you."

"You should have thought of that before you tried to play matchmaker. Does he know what you are up to?"

"No and don't you tell him either. I can't afford to lose him, not with me going on bed rest. I can't lose you either."

This was so unlike Piper. It must be all those hormones from being pregnant causing her to behave like a moron. "Fine. But only because you've been a good friend—at least until today. I will do the job and only the job. I will not go out with Derrick, no matter how cute he is."

"You think he's cute?" Her voice rose in pitch.

Hope waved a finger in the air. "Don't. It was only an observation."

"Okay. I'm sorry." Disappointment clouded her voice. "Thank you for sticking with the job. But don't overlook Derrick just because I messed up."

"Whatever." She liked Piper, but the girl was tripping. "I have work to do. Don't worry about anything here. You've assembled a good team, and your resort is in good hands."

"I agree. Don't be a stranger. I'm sure to get sick of myself, and I'll appreciate the company."

Hope grinned and shook her head. She couldn't stay mad at Piper. "I will stop in sometime soon. Catch you later." She pocketed the phone. When she arrived on the island she'd sensed it would be a different kind of place to live and work when the manager of Wildflower B&B looked troubled by her tattoos; however, she'd never imagined what Piper had in store.

She headed to her SUV. There was work to be done, and she would not spend the afternoon daydreaming. She grabbed her tools then headed inside to the north section of the resort. The sprinkler system had done its job, but the water damage was considerable in the affected rooms.

On her way through the lobby she spotted Derrick standing behind the counter. He had a Ryan Reynolds thing going on. She'd watched *The Proposal* many times over the years and had always found him attractive. Derrick's broad shoulders filled out his navy sports jacket and looked very nice, but his clean-cut boy-next-door look wasn't her thing.

Why would Piper think they'd hit it off? They were too different. She was a jeans and T-shirt girl, and he was GQ. Okay, she knew how to dress up and had to in her other life, but she much preferred her work clothes.

He looked her way and caught her staring. She whirled around and double-timed it toward the wing that needed repairs. Her cheeks burned. That would *not* happen again.

At six o'clock she called it a day, packed up, and headed to the restaurant kitchen. Looking around for the tall blonde woman Piper had described, Hope immediately spotted Zoe, the head chef, and waved as she approached.

Zoe grabbed a large brown bag. "You must be Hope. Piper called and gave me your order."

"Yes I am." She reached for her wallet.

"Your meals are complimentary for as long as you are working here."

"Really? Piper didn't tell me. Well that's a nice way to end a rough day. Thanks!"

"Sure. I heard you're staying at the Wildflower B&B."

"I am. Have you been there?"

Zoe chuckled. "My husband and I own the place. We live in the basement apartment. I'm sure our paths will cross there sooner or later."

"Small island."

"Yep. Have a nice evening. I need to get back to work."

"Okay." With her dinner bag in one hand and her toolbox in the other, she made her way to the parking lot. She spotted Derrick holding a motorcycle helmet. Well that added another dimension to Mr. GQ. She walked over to him. "You didn't stop by to check my work."

"Didn't think that was a good idea today." He winked and slipped on the helmet.

"That yours?" She looked skeptically at the Indian Chief Classic.

He straddled the seat. "Yes."

"Nice." She nodded, her curiosity piqued, but she'd never admit it to Piper. "Well, have a good night."

"Maybe I'll see you at the B&B."

"Why's that?"

"My sister's the manager, and my daughter is sort of the in-house sitter for guests. She sent me a text a little bit ago about needing to watch a kid this evening."

"Oh. Okay. Maybe I'll see you." She strode to her SUV struggling to come to terms with this new information. His sister was the uptight manager, and his daughter was old enough to babysit. How could either of those be possible? He didn't look old enough to have a teen, and he rode a motorcycle. She chuckled. His sister for sure didn't approve of that.

Wildflower Island was an interesting place. She was beginning to think she owed Piper a thank you for offering her the job. The people didn't appear as colorful on the surface as her normal crowd, but one didn't have to dig deep to see there was more to the people than met the eye.

Derrick rode past and waved. Her stomach did a little flip-flop. She couldn't go there. He was *not* her type at all, and he was a dad. She didn't date dads.

CHAPTER TWO

"I'M HOME," DERRICK CALLED OUT AS he closed the door behind him. "Alyssa?" His daughter always beat him home, but silence greeted him. He tossed his keys onto the table beside the door, slipped off his shoes, and removed his tie. "Alyssa!" He called as he strode down the hall to the right of the entrance that led to the bedrooms.

"In my room," she hollered.

He stopped outside her door. "May I come in?"

The door swung open, and his spunky daughter grinned up at him. She was as petite as her mother had been. He'd hoped she'd continue to grow, but at fifteen he figured she'd be five foot four for life. "Hi, Dad. Whoa! You look beat. Bad day?"

"An odd day. We need to talk. Things are going to get challenging for the next several months, and I'm going to need your help. Let me change, then meet me in the kitchen. We can talk while I make dinner." He continued down the hall but didn't miss the eye roll.

"That stuff you make isn't fit for human

consumption. I'm taking cooking at school and have a lot of new recipes to try. How about I start making dinner every night?"

He paused and tossed a grin over his shoulder. "That's a great idea, at least for now. We'll talk more after I change." He closed the door to his bedroom and sighed. His little girl was growing up. Not that it was a problem. After all, that's what kids were supposed to do. But was now a good time for him to take on so many hours?

Alyssa contributed so much already. Ever since Jenna had died four years ago in a car crash, his daughter had practically taken over the daily household chores.

He strode to his closet, shrugged out of his sports jacket, and in a matter of minutes, he was comfortable in his favorite pair of jeans and a gray T-shirt. He pulled a soft, black, half-zip sweatshirt over his head. Although the weather this spring had been mild, a nip hung in the air after the sun went down.

He moved into the kitchen and found Alyssa at the stove stirring something in a pot. Had she prepared dinner already? "What's this?"

"Aunt Jill must have stopped in today. I found chili in the fridge along with a note." She slid an unopened card across the brown, faux granite, Formica countertop.

He opened the card and grinned.

Happy birthday, big brother. Enjoy the chili. I used Mom's recipe. I know it's your favorite.

In the craziness of the day, he'd forgotten that today

was his thirty-sixth birthday. He glanced toward Alyssa who seemed oblivious to the fact. *Weird.* His daughter never forgot his birthday. Disappointment struck him. No, he wouldn't let her oversight get him down. After all he'd forgotten too.

He leaned over the stove and breathed in deeply. Tomatoes and the scent of warm spices made his stomach rumble. "Smells good."

"Mmm-hmm." Alyssa tapped the wooden spoon on the side of the pot, then set the table. "What did you need to talk about?"

They were going to do this now? He'd hoped to have a little food in his stomach first, but really, he was only procrastinating. "I received a temporary promotion today. I'm the acting manager at the resort until Piper returns to work after her baby is born."

Alyssa grinned. "That's great, Dad. Congratulations." She placed a pitcher of ice water in the center of the round, glass topped table in the alcove of the kitchen, then went back to the stove, removed the pot and placed it on a trivet.

He sat and waited for Alyssa to do the same then prayed a blessing over the food. "It's going to mean a lot more hours for me. I may not make it home for dinner every night, and I'll probably need to work weekends."

Her hand stopped midair as she reached for the ladle. "Like how many?"

He shrugged. "As many as needed. It's going to take some time to teach someone to do what I did. Once I get someone trained then it'll free up my time." The hesitation on her face made him frown. "What are you worried about, kiddo? You're practically an adult."

"Who can't drive. You promised to teach me now that winter is over. I know I'm signed up for Driver's Ed but I really wanted to get some hours in before the class starts."

The last thing he wanted was his fifteen-year-old daughter behind the wheel of a car, but he couldn't shelter her forever. If she could wait a few more months, her driver's training class would be over, it'd be summer, and Piper would have had her baby. Everything would be back to normal, or at least their version of normal. Jenna's death had left a gaping hole in their lives emotionally. Alyssa missed her mom and he . . . he didn't know how he felt anymore. He'd always love Jenna, but he finally felt ready to move on.

He swallowed the lump that had formed in his throat. "That's right. I did promise to teach you, but things have changed. I'm really sorry, but I don't see how I'll have time now until summer. You'll still learn to drive in your driver's training class."

"But you promised." Her voice caught.

He'd really messed up. Somehow he'd have to make this up to her. "I know, and I'm very sorry. Piper is in a bind, and I'm the only person who is able to step in and take over. Her baby's life is at stake."

Alyssa's eyes widened. "Really?"

"Unfortunately, yes." He ladled steaming chili into his bowl. He hated to disappoint his daughter, but what choice did he have? It's not like he'd planned this.

They ate the rest of the meal in silence then left the dishes in the sink and headed over to the B&B. He'd hang out there this evening with his laptop and get some work done. With the added responsibility of doing Piper's job as well as his own, he'd not had time to do everything.

Alyssa raced from her bedroom carrying a large bag that protruded on the sides.

"What's in there?"

"Supplies. You know how the kids like it when I bring coloring books and stuff."

True, but he'd not seen her take so much before. He palmed his keys and headed out to his black pickup. Then it hit him. He grinned and dangled the keys in the air. "You want to drive?"

"Really?" Her face lit.

"A promise is a promise."

She dropped the bag and gave him a bear hug. "Thank you."

He chuckled and hugged her back. "You're welcome."

She let go, picked up the bag and took the keys from him. "This is the best day ever! First I get a boyfriend, and now I get to drive."

Whoa! A boyfriend? She hadn't even mentioned liking someone. A boyfriend and driving all in the same day—ugh. What happened to his little girl? She was suddenly almost grown. If only there was a way to stop time. He stifled a groan and climbed into the passenger seat. Ten minutes later, they pulled up to the B&B.

Alyssa put the truck into park.

She turned to him. "How'd I do?"

"Not bad." She was a natural behind the wheel. Good thing too because since learning she had a boyfriend, his brain had been useless.

"I've been watching you drive so it was easy." She hopped out. "Come on, Dad. We were supposed to be here five minutes ago."

"We? I hope you don't expect me to help babysit."

She pressed her lips together. They climbed the stairs of the old Victorian house. Hanging baskets overflowing with spring flowers hung from the covered porch. A light clicked on beside the entrance. He pulled open the screen then pushed the door.

"Surprise!"

He jumped back, nearly knocking Alyssa off her feet.

The small crowd burst into a birthday song. He ambled into the dining room to the left of the entrance where his friends stood and looked around at their smiling faces. His gaze stopped at a new, but familiar face—Hope. She smiled and sang along with the rest of the group. Everyone clapped, and then Jill waved him over to the table.

"You need to blow out your candles before the cake Zoe made is covered in wax."

He hadn't even noticed the large round confection, covered in chocolate frosting—his favorite.

"Make a wish," Alyssa said.

He'd stopped making wishes a long time ago, but this time a desire he hadn't had in a long time stirred inside him. He blew out all thirty-six candles. "Thanks, everyone."

His sister sliced pieces, and before long, everyone was happily eating the melt-in-your mouth white cake with creamy chocolate frosting. He found Hope slinking up the stairs, presumably to her room. "What's your hurry?"

"No hurry." She squared her shoulders as if daring him to dispute her claim.

"There you are." Alyssa slipped her arm around his. "Aunt Jill wants you to open presents."

"Presents?"

"Well, really only one. We all chipped in."

He raised a brow toward Hope. "Help?"

She laughed. "You're on your own." He was struck by how her face transformed when she smiled. Her hazel eyes even twinkled—beautiful. He shook off the direction of his thoughts and followed Alyssa back to the dining room where she pulled a large cube-shaped box from the bag she'd brought. How had she fit that thing in there? No wonder it had looked ready to burst.

She handed it to him. A huge smile lit her face. Whatever it was, he would love it because his daughter took so much joy in presenting it to him.

He tore the wrap off the box. His stomach dropped. This was not what he expected, and he couldn't have been more surprised. It was the motorcycle helmet he'd been admiring for quite some time but didn't buy due to the hefty price tag. He looked at his daughter, then his sister, and finally his friends. "Thank you, but this is too much."

"No way, buddy," Jim, his workout partner from the gym, said. "But don't expect this kind of treatment every year."

Everyone laughed.

As it turned out, Alyssa didn't really need to babysit, and the party soon ended.

Nick, the owner of the B&B shook his hand on the way out. "Happy birthday, Derrick."

"Thanks. And thanks for letting Jill and Alyssa do this here. I never suspected a thing."

Nick grinned. "That was the idea. Jill said she's never been able to surprise you."

"True. This was a first. I should get out there before Alyssa takes off without me."

"She's driving already?" Nick shook his head. "It doesn't seem possible she's that old."

"Kind of makes you feel old too, huh?" He winked and strode to the pickup where Alyssa sat patiently waiting behind the wheel. He climbed in and buckled up.

"We sure surprised you, didn't we, Dad?"

"Yes, you did."

She backed up.

"Stop!"

She slammed on the brake. "What?"

"You almost hit that boulder." He pointed behind them.

"Oops." She adjusted the steering wheel and maneuvered out of the driveway. "So who was that cool girl you were talking to on the stairs?"

Cool? "She's from work. Piper hired her to do the electrical."

"Oh. Sounds like the two of you have a lot in common." She glanced his way. "Did you notice the tattoos on her arms? I've never seen a lady with so many."

"Lots of people have tattoos."

"Yeah, but I'm pretty sure most women don't have that much art on their arms." She gripped the wheel tighter as the lights from an oncoming vehicle shone in their faces.

His daughter exaggerated. Although Hope did have several tattoos on her arms, they weren't covered. In fact, from the elbow down, she didn't have even one.

Alyssa had lived a sheltered life, but at least she had school on the mainland. There weren't enough high school students on the island to justify a school of their own, so the teenagers were bussed to a high school off of Wildflower.

She glanced his way again. "I was thinking—"

"Eyes on the road."

"Sorry." She focused forward. "We can talk later, but my boyfriend wants to take me out for dinner and a movie. Since there's no theater on Wildflower we'd have to go to the mainland."

Alyssa knew good and well she wasn't allowed to date until she turned sixteen, but right now was not the time to get into that discussion. "Do you know who invited Hope to my birthday party?"

"I think all the guests at the B&B were invited. It was

nice of her to come."

"Yeah." Piper's warning to not judge Hope by her appearance resurfaced in his mind. It seemed his boss might have been correct when she intimated there was more to Hope than met the eye. He thought about the birthday wish he'd made. Could Hope be the answer to his wish?

Hope stared out her window at the B&B facing the Puget Sound. The ferry lights shone off in the distance. She'd been too busy to enjoy the sights since she'd arrived yesterday, but this weekend she hoped to go exploring.

She cracked the window slightly, closed the curtain, then climbed into the luxurious bed. Although the room was a little too flowery for her tastes, the bed was as comfortable as any five-star hotel's. Crickets chirped beyond her window, and the leaves rustling in the breeze soothed her frayed nerves. Today had been a Monday in every sense of the word.

Derrick and his daughter surprised her. Although she wasn't sure what she'd expected from them, their easy rapport wasn't it. Maybe her own strained relationship with her parents as a teen had clouded her expectations.

Her cell phone chimed. She pulled it from the nightstand and grinned after checking the caller ID. "Hey there, Piper."

"How was the party? Was he surprised?"

She chuckled softly at the memory of Derrick almost knocking his daughter flat. "I'd say so."

"Yes! I wish I could have been there. Jill has had this in the works for weeks. I would have given anything to see the look on his face. He is impossible to surprise."

"I don't know about that. He looked pretty shocked by me this morning."

"That's different. I blindsided you both."

"At least you admit it." Hope reached over and clicked on the bedside lamp. "How are you doing?"

"I'm bored out of my mind already! I'm not used to doing nothing but reading."

"I could teach you to knit."

"Thanks, but no thanks. Been there done that. I'm supposed to be relaxing, not getting frustrated and raising my blood pressure over dropped stitches."

Hope chuckled softly. "Have it your way. I'll stop by and visit on my way home from work tomorrow. Want me to bring you a few magazines?"

"That sounds great. All we have here are gardening magazines."

"Don't worry, my friend. I'll hook you up with some great reading." Piper wasn't the first of her friends to have a baby, and she'd learned a few things from the others. Including which books and magazines they all enjoyed. She yawned.

"I'm keeping you awake. Sorry."

"It's okay. Where's that husband of yours?" She was glad to have her friend readily available, but it wasn't like Chase not to be nearby.

"Sleeping. I'm out on the couch. I'm too restless to sleep."

"I'll be praying for you, but I need some shut-eye."

"Thanks. Goodnight."

"'Night." She laid the phone down and clicked off the light. Tomorrow should be interesting. Hopefully Mr. GQ wouldn't get in her way or slow her down.

CHAPTER THREE

Hope plopped onto a bench facing the small lake at the resort and dug into the sack lunch Zoe handed to her on the way out of the B&B this morning. Piper had done a nice job designing the resort. Rustic, yet it had all the conveniences one would expect at a five-star resort.

A wide, paved path meandered around the lake and looked like it might even venture into the woods on the other side. A couple walked hand in hand toward the boathouse where resort guests could rent paddleboats, canoes, and paddle boards. She'd always wanted to try a paddleboat. It seemed like such a silly and childish thing to do, but the child in her still wanted to.

Yellow and red tulips bloomed in a nearby planter, and pink cherry blossoms scented the air with their sweet fragrance. Good thing she didn't have allergies.

"Afternoon."

She glanced to her right. "Hi, Derrick." She ignored the quickening in her stomach. He looked the same as yesterday except today he wore a gray shirt and red tie with his black suit. She much preferred his t-shirt and jean look he had on last night.

"Mind if I join you?"

She scooted over giving him ample room. "Did you enjoy your party?"

"I did. How are things going?"

"Moving along as scheduled." A sudden thought hit her. "Is it okay that I'm out here? I mean, I don't see anyone else employed by the resort roaming around, eating."

"It's fine. Generally, Piper prefers that the contractors stay out of sight, but I believe she'd make an exception for you."

She tilted her head in his direction. "Why's that?" She didn't like special treatment, and Piper knew it.

"You aren't exactly hard to look at."

She sat up straight. "What is *that* supposed to mean?"

"It means you're not a dude with a scruffy face, hard hat and low riding jeans. You are put together, for the most part."

She raised a brow. "The most part?" One minute he sounded like he was complimenting her, and the next he was delivering an insult.

His face matched the color of his tie. He was obviously flustered, but he did this to himself. Didn't he realize as the acting manager that he needed to choose his words more carefully?

He tilted his head and sighed. "I'm really messing this up. Please don't be offended by my bumbling. I'm trying to say having you out in the public spaces of the resort would not bother the guests because you are attractive and not walking around in dirty work clothes."

"Oh." She looked down at her jeans and noted she'd inadvertently worn her nicest pair, along with a black, long sleeved Henley under a nice purple T-shirt she'd picked up at the resort gift shop this morning when she'd purchased the promised magazines for Piper. She'd forgotten to pack her uniform shirt when she came to the island and had to make do with regular clothes. Her cheeks heated. "Thank you. I let my crew do the dirty work." She shot him a cheeky grin.

"Mmm-hmm. Me too." He pried the lid off a dish and spooned a bite of chili into his mouth.

"Are you eating that cold?" Her stomach roiled at the thought.

"No. There's a microwave in the office. If you ever need to use it, you're welcome to."

"More special treatment?"

He nodded. "You're the boss's friend. Enjoy it."

Hope almost laughed. Piper was probably doing anything she could to make sure she stayed on the job. Well, she need not worry, because Hope needed this job more than she cared to admit, and was thankful she hadn't followed through with her threat to quit. That would have been a huge mistake.

She bit into the ham and cheese sandwich. Rather than question all the nice things Piper was making happen, she would enjoy the special treatment. And make sure Piper had nothing to worry about. Her friend worked hard and needed this time to take care of herself and her unborn child. "Did you ride to work today?"

He grinned. "On a day like today? Need you ask?"

She laughed. "How's the new helmet?"

"Perfect. How'd you know about that?"

"Your friends were talking about it before you got to the party. They were pretty excited to give it to you." It must be nice to have so many trusted people to count on. She allowed few people that privilege. After what happened with her mother, she lost her faith in the goodness of people.

"Yeah? I felt like they overdid the gift, but knowing it made them so happy helps me feel better. Thanks."

"Sure." Hope finished off her lunch and stood. "Think I'll get back to work."

Derrick nodded. "I'll stop in and look things over before I head out today."

She frowned. So he really did plan to look over her shoulder. She clamped her teeth together to keep from saying something she shouldn't and marched inside.

A few hours later she sensed someone in the suite with her and looked over her shoulder. "Hey, Derrick. I'm about finished here."

"Don't let me rush you."

I won't. She tightened the screw, backed away, and with a flourish of her arms motioned toward the wall. "It's all yours." She stepped aside as he casually looked at the wiring for the jetted tub.

"Looks good to me."

She let out her breath in a whoosh. "Good. Now I'll be able to sleep."

He chuckled. "I'm only doing my job."

"So am I. See you tomorrow." She grabbed all of her stuff and strode from the room. Maybe Derrick wouldn't turn out to be a nuisance on the jobsite after all. But the idea he was assigned to check her work, so Piper could play matchmaker still irked her.

"I appreciate your situation, Hope, but this isn't open for debate." Piper sat propped up in her bed with arms crossed. A white down comforter folded halfway back revealed she wore yoga pants. Clearly she had no intention of living in bedclothes for the next several months.

Hope sat beside her friend's bed. "I've never known you to be so unreasonable. Why are you doing this?"

"It's not that I don't trust you, but I already asked Derrick to double check your work, and I don't want to look indecisive in my assistant manager's eyes. It's bad enough I can't do my job right now. I can't afford to lose the respect of my employees."

Hope pulled the magazines she'd brought out of her bag and gently tossed them within Piper's reach. "I hear what you're saying, but I doubt the people who work for you would think less of you if you change a request. Especially Derrick. He seems like a reasonable person and a genuinely nice man."

"He is, but please just go with me on this."

Hope stood and paced Piper's bedroom. "You have an amazing view of the Sound from here."

"I know. I'm so glad Chase chose well when he bought the place. I love it, even if it is a little on the small side." Piper cleared her throat. "So, how are you doing? Have you made any sculptures lately?"

Hope tensed and kept her focus on the water. Piper knew good and well the humiliation and pain her manager/mother had inflicted on her. She'd left the art world and had zero intention of ever returning. "No. That part of my life is over."

"It doesn't have to be. I know your mom hurt you when you overheard that conversation, but it doesn't mean she was right. You are a talented artist."

Hope sucked in a breath. Piper didn't know the half of it, nor would she. Hope did not like talking about her mom's stint as her manager. A mom should never say the cruel things she'd overheard her say or steal from her daughter. Her mother's greed had removed any desire to create from then forward. Hope had not even drawn a new design since that day.

She turned back to her friend. "I appreciate your kind words, but why does it matter to you?"

"I like your work and want to add to my collection. Did you notice the windmill in the garden at the resort? It's one of yours."

Her eyes widened. "I haven't explored much."

"I also have one of your wind chimes."

Why was Piper doing this? She knew her art was a painful topic.

"I'd like to commission you to create a sculpture that would hang on the boathouse. I'm thinking something whimsical with a bird. Maybe a stork." She chuckled. "You get it? A stork?"

Hope offered a grin, but couldn't muster a laugh. "I get it, and although I'm flattered, I'll pass. I should be going." She stood and hugged Piper. "Will Chase be home soon?"

She nodded. "He's bringing dinner. I'm sure there's plenty if you want to hang out here tonight."

"Thanks, but Zoe handed me a boxed dinner on my way out again. I appreciate you arranging that."

"You're welcome. I figured it was the least I could do since I'm cramping your style." She grinned sheepishly.

"I agree." She shot back playfully. She'd missed these times. They'd been roommates in college and had spent many hours talking into the wee hours of the morning then half-sleeping through classes the next day. Her parents insisted she go to college and get a degree in business management. She hadn't cared much for traditional school and wanted to go to a trade school instead, but her parents won her over to their side when they offered to pay for everything.

It all worked out in the end. She still went to trade school following college, and started tinkering with metal art on the side. And she had a degree that helped her know how to run her businesses. A win-win as her dad had said on numerous occasions.

"How do you like Wildflower B&B?"

"It's nice, and the food Zoe makes is some of the

best I've ever had. If I'm not careful, I'm going to gain ten pounds while I'm here."

Piper chuckled. "I agree. Did I mention that while the resort was being built, I occupied the same room as you?"

"Nope. Funny coincidence."

"Not really. They've dubbed the Poppy room their long-term guest room. Nick, the owner, finally decided after numerous long-term guests stayed, to set a by-the-month rate for that room."

"Hmm. Speaking of the B&B, I should head out."

"Okay. Thanks for the magazines and please consider my request for a sculpture. Regardless of what happened with your mom, you are the best metal artist around, and I would love to have another piece by the famous H.L."

"Shh!" Her heart raced.

Piper laughed. "No one can hear me."

"True, but you know that I want anonymity. Sure, people recognized me back when I was sculpting, but no one here has a clue about my past, and I'd like it to stay that way. If anyone recognizes that name and puts two and two together . . ." She shivered. "I can't deal with all the questions about what happened to me and whether the rumors are true." In certain circles, she had been quite the celebrity, and keeping her pseudonym secret protected her privacy.

"Don't worry. No one here has even heard of H.L., and they'd never put two and two together."

That was at least some comfort, but still . . . She had

no desire to pick up where she'd left off. It was all too painful. "Take care of yourself." She gave Piper a quick hug and darted out the door, passing Chase on his way in. "Hey, Chase."

"You leaving?"

"Yep. I've been here a while. Catch you later." Fresh air and a run were in order, and she knew exactly the place to clear her head.

Thirty minutes later, wearing a headlamp, since the sun was setting and the beach was not lit, Hope jogged down around the side of the B&B to the backyard and followed the path that led to the beach. She ducked to avoid a low hanging branch. Her pulse increased slightly as the water came into view.

Pebbles beneath her feet shifted slightly as she found her running rhythm. Soon she barely noticed the fluctuating surface and instead enjoyed the gentle breeze that cooled her neck. She'd taken up running after quitting metal art. Her mom had pressured her so much to produce something new after she'd learned what her mother had been up to that she'd turned to running as a form of escape. She learned quickly to turn off her phone since Mom would never slip on running shoes to join her. Eventually she had accepted that Hope was finished with art.

At least Hope thought she was finished. She owed Piper a lot. Could she go there again and create the piece her friend wanted?

Piper's request unsettled her, and she couldn't get it out of her mind. Her friend knew what happened. Knew how devastated she'd been when she discovered her mother had been stealing from her, even though she'd been paid a twenty percent commission on everything Hope sold. On top of that, she had spread rumors that Hope was an alcoholic, driven to drink by her passion for her craft—a misguided attempt to attract more attention to Hope's work.

The crazy thing was, she didn't even like the taste of alcohol. Mom was a master at mind games—still was—but Hope knew better now and kept her distance as much as possible.

Hope suddenly tripped and stumbled to the ground, landing on all fours, jarring her arms. The light on her head flew off and went out. Shrouded in darkness she reached out for the headlamp and only found pebbles and something wet and slimy—Ewe! She jerked her hand back. Her stomach lurched as unease settled over her. It was funny how that small light made such a huge difference in her view of things.

She slowly stood and gazed toward the water as it lapped against the shoreline. Soon her eyes adjusted to the light of the nearly full moon and stars. Beautiful. The headlamp rested on the pebbles a few feet away. She grabbed it and flipped the tiny switch—nothing. She tried again, still nothing. Now what?

How far had she run? It wouldn't be easy to run back without the light, but nature's lamp would do. Turning in the direction she'd come, she walked off the pain from the fall then sped up to an easy jog. The farther she jogged the more concerned she became. Everything looked the same. Would she recognize the pathway that led to the B&B if she saw it? Would she even see it? Staying on the beach all night didn't appeal.

She kept on for what seemed like forever. Surely she'd run out of beach sooner or later. A person holding a flashlight walked in her direction. Unease gripped her—what if the person was trouble? Not likely here on Wildflower. But thankfully her dad had taught her self-defense should the need arise.

"There you are."

"Derrick?" Relief washed through her. "What are you doing here? Not that I'm complaining. I'm a little lost."

"Jill was concerned and asked me to see if I could find you."

"She did?" That seemed so unlike the B&B manager. Then again, the woman went out of her way to make sure the guests were comfortable and content. "What time is it?"

"Around nine."

Her stomach did a flip-flop. "I didn't realize I was out so long. I'm sorry for worrying her and causing you to come look for me, but I'm really glad you did. I didn't know where the pathway was that led back to the B&B." It chagrined her to admit it, but she wanted him to know she appreciated what he did.

"It's not a problem. It's a little tricky finding the path at night. Do you usually take such long runs?"

"No. At least not at night." She bent her right leg and grasped her ankle then repeated the process with her left one. "I asked Jill how to get down to the beach because I'd wanted to clear my head. I guess I lost track of time." Plus her tumble slowed her down. She shook her head. "I can't believe your sister worried about me."

He chuckled. "Jill is a very nice person once you get to know her, but she does come across as uptight to some people."

Hope chuckled. "You mean she's not?"

He laughed. "She can be. You ready to head back?"

"Yes." The cool air hitting her damp skin caused gooseflesh to rise, and she shivered. "Brr. It gets cold at night."

Derrick shrugged off his jacket and draped it over her shoulders.

"Thanks." She breathed in the musky scent on the fabric. She didn't recognize the cologne, a combination of citrus and spice—very nice.

"Sure. My wife was a runner too. She often forgot to bring warm enough clothes for her cool-down and came home shivering." He shined the light on their path. "I noticed you're carrying a light, but not using it."

"Yeah. It broke when I fell and it flew off my head." She wanted to ask him about his wife, but held back.

"Sounds painful."

"A little." She shrugged and ducked under the same branch she'd encountered on the way down to the beach. "You said Jill was concerned about me and here I thought she didn't like me."

"Really? I couldn't say one way or the other. Tonight is the first time you were brought up."

"Then you think she might not?" Something about

his tone and evasiveness made her think she was right. "Why wouldn't she like me? I've been polite, I keep my room tidy, and I chew with my mouth closed."

He laughed.

"It's not funny."

"Yes, it is," he said while still chuckling. "You don't know my sister well, but you nailed her pet peeves."

Hope grinned. Okay, so maybe that was a little funny. The B&B's well-lit property came into view as they left the path into the backyard.

Jill stepped out the back door. "There you are. I was worried." She wore a sweater tugged closed that hung almost to her knees.

"Sorry, I wasn't paying attention to the time. I'm not used to people watching after me."

"No need to apologize. I'm glad you're okay. I guess I panicked for no reason. I should head inside."

"'Night, sis." He guided them around the side of the house to the front porch. "I need to get home. I left Alyssa doing homework, but I have a feeling the minute I walked out the door, she was Skyping with her boyfriend, Gabe."

"She has a boyfriend?"

"Her first." He frowned, clearly not pleased with the situation.

"How sweet. Have you met him?"

"No. I learned about him the same day my hours jumped."

She nodded. "Don't worry, Dad. I'm sure you raised a smart daughter." She handed him his jacket and instantly chilled. "Thanks again. See you tomorrow."

She wanted to dislike the man because of Piper's matchmaking antics, but he was making it very difficult.

CHAPTER FOUR

THE FOLLOWING WEEK, DERRICK SAT AT his desk in the office situated behind reception at the resort. It felt like a Monday, but it was Wednesday. Things were not going well at home. He could still hear Alyssa shouting at him that he didn't care about her and that her boyfriend loved her. A boy he still hadn't met.

Somehow meeting the kid would make it too real. He wasn't ready for this stage of his daughter's life.

The office door swung open, and Chase sauntered in wearing his typical garb, Levis and a flannel shirt. A little casual for the resort, but considering he generally worked on the grounds, his attire was appropriate.

Chase stuck out a fist. "Thought I'd find you here."

Derrick bumped it. "Hey, man. How's Piper?" His boss's husband was a great guy. Very down to earth. He enjoyed it when Chase stopped in.

"Going crazy, but otherwise fine."

"Good. I didn't imagine bed rest would suit her well."

Chase chuckled. "Nope. How are things going here? Anything I need to deal with?"

"It's been a challenge taking over for Piper, but I have everything handled. Is there anything I can help with?"

"Nope. Take it easy. I'll check in with you in a day or two. Call if something comes up."

"Will do." He grinned as the man left the office. Piper said her husband would be by twice a day, but clearly Chase was his own man and did things his way.

"Knock. Knock."

He looked toward the doorway leading to the reception area, and his gut twisted. "Hi, Hope. Come in." For some reason, his daughter had taken an instant liking to Hope and admired her tattoos. Now Alyssa wanted a tattoo in the shape of a heart with her boyfriend's and her name. The idea was bad on so many levels, but he couldn't get her to understand.

"I got your message. What's up?" Hope asked, completely unaware of the turmoil she was causing in his house, thanks to her tattoos.

"How much longer until the work is completed in the north wing?"

"It's going to take a while. We have to rip everything out room-by-room and start from scratch. It was a mess in there."

He knew she was right. He'd seen the water damage.

"If we push hard and everything falls into place, we might be finished by next Friday, but that is the best case scenario."

He squared his shoulders. "Really? That's great news." He'd been so busy dealing with everything else, he'd neglected to oversee Hope's work. He'd make sure to check it before heading out tonight.

"Is that all you wanted?"

"Yes. Thanks for stopping by."

"You could have sent me a text."

"I prefer to do things in person."

She nodded and looked at him closely. "Are you okay? You don't seem yourself."

"Rough morning."

"Work?"

He started to shake his head, but it had been a little rocky here too. "Mostly I'm learning to be the dad of a teenage girl."

"Isn't she fifteen? I'd have thought you would've figured that out by now."

"Spoken like someone with no kids."

She chuckled. "I was a teen girl once. What seems to be the problem?" She leaned against the doorjamb.

As much as he appreciated the offer of help, he didn't care to admit that her tattoos were the problem. Plus, he'd been taking care of Alyssa on his own for four years now, and until the past week or so things had gone well, at least for the most part. The time right after Jenna's accident had been really rough. "It's nothing."

"Suit yourself, but if you change your mind you know where to find me." She spun around and left.

Great, one more person annoyed with him. He stewed for a moment then stood and followed after her, catching her in the hall. "Hope, wait."

She stopped. "I need to get to work if you want that

wing finished by next week."

"Understood. May I walk with you?" Yep, she was clearly miffed considering a minute ago she had plenty of time to listen to him. "As you know, Alyssa has a boyfriend—her first. He's a senior, and she's only a sophomore."

"Strike one." She made a slash in the air.

He grinned. "I've always told her she couldn't date until she turned sixteen. He wants to take her to the mainland for dinner and a movie." He wouldn't bring up the tattoos, as there was no sense dragging her into the mire of his daughter's drama.

"That's sweet."

"Sweet?" His voice rose slightly. "He probably only has one thing on his mind."

"Maybe, but don't you trust your daughter?"

"Of course I do—at least, in regard to most things, but I don't trust this punk."

She glanced his way with a raised brow. "So you've met him?"

"Well, no."

"Parents," she said with mock disgust. "How can you call the guy a punk when you haven't even met? That's not very fair. And, you're not exactly showing your daughter that you trust her when you pre-judge the guy she cares about. What kind of message is that sending her?"

He hadn't thought of that. "Oh."

"And while I'm at it. When you do meet him, don't assume you know him based on his appearance. Take the time to get acquainted with the real person. People misjudge me all the time. They think I'm some tough chick because I'm an electrician and I have a few tattoos. They don't even see *me*."

"You mean you're not a tough chick?" He quirked a grin.

"Very funny." She rolled her eyes. "I'm tough, but not the kind of person they imagine." She stopped at the entrance of the room she was working in.

He liked this side of Hope. Piper's warning not to judge a book by its cover came to mind. Now he knew without a doubt what she was hinting at.

"Look, I get why you don't want your daughter dating a senior, and why you told her she couldn't date until she was sixteen, but you are going to lose her if you don't come to some kind of compromise."

"Are you speaking from personal experience? Your parents didn't like the guys you dated?" Hope intrigued him. The more time he spent with her the more he wanted to get to know her. Even if she was unknowingly causing him trouble at home.

"Let's just say we did not see eye-to-eye on many things. They were too strict, and I rebelled, which is exactly what Alyssa might do if you don't come to a compromise you can both be happy with. Why not invite her boyfriend over for a supervised date? They can have dinner at your place and watch a movie there."

He nodded. "That might work. Thanks." He gently squeezed her shoulder. "For the record, I think you turned out fine." Even if she worked in a field traditionally dominated by men. He admired her for her success.

"I'll send you my bill," she teased. "Oh, and no hovering. She'll think you don't trust her."

He nodded and sauntered back to his office. Hope could be onto something. Maybe he'd even like the kid once he met him—fat chance.

Hope's shoulder tingled where Derrick's hand had been. Why did she have such a reaction to this man? He was nothing like the usual men she dated. His standard work attire was a *suit,* for starters. The guys that attracted her wore jeans and motorcycle boots to work. Then again, he rode a motorcycle. There was more to Derrick than met the eye, but was she willing to risk getting to know him?

She was no stranger to heartbreak and wasn't sure she was up to more should Derrick not turn out to be the kind of man she suspected he was. Then again, Piper was certain they'd hit it off, and she knew Hope better than anyone. Or at least she had.

They'd been friends for years and had confided a lot to each other when in college, but that was a long time ago. She wasn't that young girl anymore. She'd grown up and gotten rid of the stars in her eyes. It was still hard to believe she used to be a semi-famous metal sculpture artist. Which reminded her, Piper was still on her case about that sign for the boathouse.

She had no idea what to do about that either since Piper refused to take no for an answer. But for now, she needed to focus on her job.

The day flew by, and before it seemed possible, she was gathering her belongings. "Good work today, Todd. I'm hoping to wrap this wing up by the end of next week."

"Ha! Not likely, unless you bring in another crew."

She nodded. He was right, and she'd already planned to pull the crew working on the cabins into the hotel.

"Good evening." Derrick walked into the room. He'd lost the suit jacket and tie and wore a white shirt rolled up to his elbows.

"What brings you by?" she asked.

"I need to check what you've done. Piper won't be happy with me if I don't."

"Right. I forgot about that."

A few minutes later he came back into the main room. "Looks textbook. The boss will be pleased."

"Did you expect anything less?" she teased.

"No." He rubbed the back of his neck. "I feel like I need to tell you something."

She stood to her full height. "Okay." He looked as nervous as a man on his wedding day. Unease gripped her. "Don't keep me in suspense."

He shook his head. "Not here. Jill invited Alyssa and me to dinner at the B&B tonight. She's hoping to get alone time with Alyssa and see what's going on with her. While they're visiting, maybe you and I could go for a walk on the beach or we could run, if you prefer."

Curiosity piqued, she nodded. "That would be fine."

"Great. I'll text you when I'm ready."

"I thought you didn't do that."

"In this case it makes more sense than a phone call. Don't you agree?" Without waiting for a reply, he continued. "May I walk you out?"

They left the suite, and she closed the door behind them. "I need to stop by the kitchen before leaving. Piper has arranged to have all my meals provided by the restaurant. Let me tell you, I've never eaten so well. Zoe is quite the chef."

"That's great." He stopped where she would head in a different direction. "I'll see you later then."

"Yep." She watched for a moment as he strode out the sliding glass doors into the fading sunlight, then pulled her gaze away and hustled to the kitchen. Zoe stood near the stove, talking with a dark-haired woman with pale skin. She walked over to them. "Hi, Zoe. Is my meal ready?"

Zoe looked her way and grinned. "Hope, you haven't met Rachel yet. She's my sous chef, and I predict she will one day be a top chef with a restaurant of her own."

Pink immediately stained Rachel's pale cheeks. "It's nice to meet you, Hope. I hear you are staying in the Poppy room at the B&B. That's where I first stayed when I came to this island. Met my husband at the B&B too."

Zoe grinned wider. "They just had their first baby in December. Sophia is a doll."

Rachel's face softened. "She is such a good baby,

and Chris is an exceptional dad." She looked at Hope. "He works from home, so he's pretty much a stay-at-home dad and loving it."

Someday Hope wanted to have kids, but that day didn't look to be near.

"I met my husband there too," Zoe said.

"Wow. The Wildflower Bed-and-Breakfast should advertise as a romantic destination." Hope raised her arm and moved her hand horizontally as she said, "Stay at Wildflower B&B and meet your mate."

Zoe and Rachel laughed.

"But seriously," Zoe said, "it seems like everyone who stays in that room ends up living here permanently."

Not Hope. She had a home in Tacoma and had no intention of moving here.

Zoe and Rachel looked at each other and shared a secret smile.

"What am I missing?"

"Nothing," Zoe said. "Though you are closer to the truth about the B&B than you realize. How are things going for you? Are you enjoying your downtime? I assume you aren't working twenty-four-seven."

"I work normal hours." In truth she'd been kind of lonely. She didn't socialize with her crew, and she didn't want to tire Piper by stopping in for a visit every evening. "It's almost dark by the time I leave so I spend most evenings in my room. Although I did take a run on the beach the other night."

Zoe nodded. "I heard about that."

Rachel moved a pot off the stove. "Excuse me, I need to take care of this."

"No problem. It was nice meeting you." Though quiet, Rachel seemed nice. Hope turned her attention back to Zoe as she handed her the sack containing her dinner. "I need to get busy too. I prepared beef stroganoff. It's still a little chilly out so I thought you might enjoy some comfort food. There's also steamed vegetables and a side salad. For dessert, triple chocolate cake."

"Oh my. I'm going to gain ten pounds before I leave the island."

Zoe chuckled. "Not likely, if you keep running."

Hope wanted to ask why Jill had been so concerned about her, but clearly Zoe was too busy to visit any longer. "Thanks for the meal. See you tomorrow." She waved to Rachel and left.

On the drive to the B&B her thoughts turned to Derrick. What did he want to talk about? She couldn't imagine what it was, but it seemed personal. Good thing Zoe had made comfort food. She definitely needed it tonight.

CHAPTER FIVE

Derrick clicked on his flashlight and led the way down the path from the B&B to the pebble-covered beach. He could hear Hope's soft footfalls behind him and the occasional twig snapping.

"I'm stuffed," Hope said. "Zoe made me a dinner that could have fed two people, and of course I ate it all."

He chuckled. "I don't blame you. I've had her food, and it's fantastic. Walking sounds perfect. I overate too. My sister made us lasagna."

"Sounds good. So what is it you'd like to talk with me about?" She strolled up beside him as they exited the pathway.

He walked near the shoreline. Water lapped close to his feet. Unease about the topic he'd chosen settled on him. Maybe this was a bad idea after all. He didn't know Hope that well. What if he offended her and made working with her more strained than it already was? He wasn't in the habit of taking his problems to others—especially women. But bad idea or not, he'd come this far and really needed advice. He looked toward her, her profile dim thanks to the extra dark night. "I wanted to talk with you about Alyssa."

"Your daughter?" Surprise lit her voice and sounded too loud in the serene setting.

"Yes. It seems she admires you. I don't know why since she's only met you once."

"Thanks a lot," she said dryly.

"Sorry. That's not how I meant it."

"Mmm-hmm. Actually she's been at the B&B a few times since I've arrived. Your sister brought her over."

This was news to him, but he'd worked late a couple of nights and also put in several hours over the weekend. His sister had been stepping in to help since his wife's death. Now that he knew they'd spent time together, Alyssa's obsession with Hope made more sense.

Hope rested a hand on his arm. "Are you okay?"

"Yes, sorry. Just lost in thought." *Here goes nothing.* "The thing is my daughter thinks you're cool and talks about you all the time. She wants to be like you."

"What's wrong with that? You said yourself I turned out okay."

"Yes, but she wants a tattoo." Even to his own ears he sounded pathetic.

"Don't worry, Dad. The law is on your side in this case. It's illegal for her to get a tattoo until she turns eighteen in Washington State, even with parental consent."

He did a fist pump. "Yes! How'd you know?"

"I wanted to get one at her age too but couldn't. On my eighteenth birthday I got my first. Shine your light here." She pulled the collar of the shirt slightly off her shoulder and pointed to a tiny rose.

"It's small."

She chuckled. "Well, once I got to the tattoo parlor I was a little afraid. The artist said she could make it small. So I went with it. It's a nice reminder of the day I became an adult. I celebrated several other birthdays with a new tattoo until I turned thirty, then I stopped. Most of them are inspirational sayings."

He nodded. "So which one did you get on your twenty-first birthday?"

"That was not a good year. I still regret that night. You're going to laugh."

"I promise I won't." He'd never seen Hope act so uneasy. Whatever this tattoo was it must be a whopper.

She groaned. "I can't believe I'm going to tell you."

He flashed the light so he could see her face better. What kind of tattoo would have her looking so uncomfortable?

"My friends and I had watched *Pirates of the Caribbean*, I'd had my first drink ever—"

"Hold on. Ever?" He shined the light on her face again. She looked annoyed.

"Yes. I tried my first drink that night and got tipsy. Now stop shining that thing in my face. Do you want to hear this or not?"

"Sorry. Continue."

"Anyhow. I was a little tipsy. I had a crush on

Captain Jack Sparrow and well . . ." Her voice dropped near a whisper. "I got a tattoo of his face."

"Come again? It sounded like you said Captain Jack Sparrow is forever inked on you." That was one tattoo he'd enjoy seeing if he'd heard her correctly.

"It is Captain Jack. Okay? Now let's talk about something else."

"Oh no. You don't drop something like that and expect to switch topics. This is big. Where is it?"

"My upper back."

No wonder he had never seen it. But boy would he like to. "May I have a peek?"

"Seriously?" Her voice hitched. "No!"

"Ah. Come on. One quick look. Please?" He drew out the word. "I happen to be a fan of the movie."

"No way." She crossed her arms and picked up the pace.

He lengthened his stride to match her pace. "It's a shame you went through all of that, and no one even gets to enjoy it."

"You're relentless." She sighed. "Fine. But if you ever breathe a word about this to anyone . . ." She dipped the neck of her shirt down revealing a masterful tattoo that must have been quite expensive, given the details. The colors, at least what he could see with the flashlight, were fantastic too.

"You shouldn't hide that. It's perfect. Any regrets?"

She quickly adjusted her shirt. "Let's just say, I didn't consider the consequences of my actions that night and now keep that tattoo covered at all times."

"Not a Captain Jack fan anymore?"

"I still like him, but I didn't realize people would judge me for having a drunken pirate inked onto my back."

He chuckled.

"You promised you wouldn't laugh." She nudged his shoulder, causing him to sidestep.

"Sorry, but it's ironic that you had a drunken pirate permanently etched onto your body the night you were *slightly* inebriated."

"That was the one and only time I ever drank. After that night, I learned my lesson. Apparently I make poor choices under the influence."

"At least you learned from your mistake. I think that's the problem I'm having with Alyssa. She's not thinking through the consequences of the things she wants."

"Perhaps, but I wouldn't worry too much. She's way more levelheaded than I was at her age. Remember when I told you my parents were strict and I rebelled?"

"Yes."

"Well, I wasn't exaggerating. Thankfully getting good grades was important to me, or who knows where I would have ended up."

"Sounds serious." He barely made out her shrug in the light of the moon.

"Some of it was, but nothing illegal. I wasn't out to ruin my life, simply make my parents miserable."

By the sound of it, he had it pretty good with Alyssa. They only needed to get through this boyfriend thing.

"Did any of your trouble with your parents involve boys?" He quickly added, "If I'm getting too personal, forget I asked that."

"Normally I would say you are, but under the circumstances I get where the question comes from. To answer you, yes. But that's all I'm saying. I'd be happy to reach out to Alyssa. She's a sweet girl. Maybe I can help steer her in the right direction. I could come over sometime and help her with her homework or something."

He hesitated. What would it be like to have another woman in his house? He liked Hope. She was easy to talk to, and he appreciated her honesty. What was his problem? It wasn't like they were dating or anything. They were friends. Surely it wasn't a big deal to have her over. "I think that might work since she looks up to you. When would you like to come over?"

"I'm not sure yet. Let me think on it, and I'll let you know. I'm not even sure the homework angle will work."

He stopped. "We should probably head back. I don't want Jill to worry." They reversed course.

"What's up with your sister anyway?"

"Jill's always been sensitive and uptight, thanks to a couple of incidents, my wife's fatal car crash being one of them. She panics when people are later than expected."

"Oh. That's not a fun way to live."

"Nope. It's not easy on anyone in her life either, but she's doing much better than she used to."

"Progress is good."

He had a feeling Hope understood better than she was letting on. The path leading to the B&B was a few feet ahead on their left. "Thanks for helping me with my daughter. I was afraid I was going to offend you again."

"Again?"

"You know, like when I looked over your work."

"Oh, that." She waved a hand as if it was inconsequential.

He chuckled and shined the light onto the path. "Here we go." His cell phone rang. "Hello?"

"Dad, when are you getting back? I have homework."

"We're almost there." He wanted to point out that she'd had all afternoon to do her homework but kept Hope's advice in mind and let it slide.

"Jill?" Hope asked after he hung up.

"No, Alyssa. She's in a hurry to go home and do homework." Something small flew past them so close he could feel the air from its wings. He caught a glimpse of a tiny bat.

Hope screamed and grabbed his arm. "What was that?" She clung to him.

"I'm guessing a little brown bat."

"Oh. Nooo." She shook her head, dropped her hold on his arm and did a squeamish kind of jig. "I hate bats." She sprinted toward the B&B.

Derrick ran after her and burst from the path right as Hope toppled over a lawn chair. He rushed to her side. "Are you hurt?"

"Only my pride." She rolled over and stood. "Bats

are about the only creature on earth that I can't handle. I was in such a hurry to get away, that I wasn't paying enough attention."

"It doesn't help that one of the lights on the house burned out. It's a little darker than usual back here." He clasped her hand without thinking, but since she didn't pull away he kept it fully enveloped. She trembled beneath his grasp. His heart warmed toward this multi-faceted woman. "I'm sure it was only a little brown bat," he said in the soothing voice he used with Alyssa when she was upset. "We probably were attracting insects with our body heat, and it was looking for food."

He quickly guided them to the front entrance and went inside, releasing her hand as they crossed the threshold.

Alyssa stood there waiting. Her eyes widened. "What happened, Hope? You have grass stains on your jeans."

Hope shrugged. "I got a little freaked out by a bat and wasn't paying attention to where I was going. No big deal." She turned to Derrick. Pink tinged her cheeks. "Thanks for getting me inside safely. I don't think I'll be taking any more after dark walks or runs." She shivered. "If you'll excuse me, I need a hot shower." She darted up the stairs.

Alyssa giggled softly. "She's really afraid of bats."

"What gave you that idea?" He mussed up her hair.

"Dad!" she whined. "Don't do that."

"Oops." He held back a grin that threatened to give away how much he enjoyed teasing her. Maybe he'd worried over nothing, and things with Alyssa would go back to normal.

"So I was talking with Gabe while you were out."

So much for things going back to normal.

After her shower Hope sank into a comfy chair in her room at the Wildflower B&B with a cup of decaffeinated coffee in her hands and cradled her cell phone between her neck and shoulder. "How are you doing, Piper?" Talking to Piper should get her mind off of Derrick.

"My doctor says everything looks good."

"That's not what I meant. How are *you* doing?"

"Oh. Well, I'm bored and antsy. I can't believe I have close to two-and-a-half more months of this."

"Me either." By the sound of Piper's voice, Hope suspected her friend needed a serious diversion.

"How are things with you and Derrick?"

Now there was a loaded question if she ever heard one. A crick in her neck began to hurt. She set the coffee mug on a side table and grasped the phone in her hand. "I don't appreciate that he looks over my work, but I blame you for that. He's actually a sweet man." Who she couldn't get out of her head! "I called to talk about you. Not Derrick."

"Too bad," Piper said with a playful tone. "He's nice, huh? I knew the two of you would hit it off." She cleared her throat. "Chase heard through the grapevine at the resort that you two are friendly."

"Oh good grief. We are polite and professional at the resort. I don't know what people think they saw." However, he was very friendly tonight and not the least bit professional. She still couldn't believe he'd held her hand. Then again, she'd been slightly traumatized. He was probably only trying to make her feel better, and his taking her hand meant nothing.

"Only polite? Come on, I know you. And I know him. There must be more."

Instead of getting annoyed like she wanted to do, Hope considered how bored her friend was and decided to show mercy. "He's having problems with his daughter and asked me for advice."

"You're kidding. Derrick is such a private man. This is going better than I expected. What did you do to get him to open up to you?"

"Nothing. If you were here, he probably would have talked to you instead."

"Not a chance. We have a strictly professional relationship and never discuss personal topics."

Typical Piper. The walls she put up could rival the Great Wall of China. Then again, since coming to this island, she'd seen the softer side of her friend surface more often than not. "You're his boss. He probably isn't comfortable talking about anything not related to work."

"I agree. So what kind of advice did you give him?"

"Nothing major. I told him a little bit of my upbringing and how I rebelled. Tossed in a few words of wisdom from a daughter's point of view and left the rest up to him." Piper didn't need to know she told him about her Captain Jack tattoo. She rarely told anyone about it. If she had it to do over, she'd have done something more sedate, like a nice floral design. Yes, she had a thing for flowers, but at that time in her life she had a thing for *Pirates of the Caribbean* and specifically Captain Jack.

"How'd he take it?"

"My advice? Fine, I guess. It was really no big deal." Now, his taking her hand at the end of their walk felt like a big deal, but then again, she'd been upset. He was probably trying to comfort her, like he would his daughter—not that she was young enough to be his daughter. They were probably only a few years apart in age.

"Hmm."

"What?"

"Nothing. Just hmm."

"Fine. If you're going to be like that, I'm hanging up. You can be bored by yourself."

"I'm not by myself. Chase is here."

Hope rolled her eyes. "Good night. Tell Chase I said hi." She disconnected the call then padded into the bathroom and brushed her teeth. Tonight had been nice up to the point of the bat and subsequently falling and embarrassing herself. Could Piper's matchmaking skills be as good as her sense of business?

Not that it mattered since Derrick had shown no sign of being interested in her as anything more than a friend. Besides, he probably was one of those one-woman kind of men who married once and never again. Otherwise he'd have re-married by now. Wouldn't he?

Four years was a long time to stay single if he didn't want to.

Or perhaps he hadn't met the right woman.

CHAPTER SIX

Friday evening after work, Derrick meandered through the hall leading to the north wing that Hope had been working in. They'd completed work yesterday, but he hadn't had a chance to check it out yet. He nodded to an older couple dressed for a night out. Wildflower Fresh, the resort's signature restaurant, hosted a concert from seven to nine on Friday evenings. This week a popular Jazz band from Seattle was performing.

He'd love to stay and listen, but Gabe was coming over tonight. Alyssa had agreed to the compromise, since he'd explained he wanted to get to know her boyfriend before he considered letting her date him.

He stopped in front of the room and heard arguing inside. That was odd. No one should be in there. He slid the keycard in the slot and pushed inside.

A man who looked to be in his early twenties held Hope's arm in a vise grip. Derrick fisted his hands. "Hey!" His adrenaline spiked, and he strode toward them. "What's going on in here?"

"None of your business," the man said through

clenched teeth.

Derrick stepped closer, causing the guy to shift back a step. "This is very much my business. I'm the manager here, and you're not supposed to be in this room. Who are you, and what do you think you're doing?" He looked pointedly at the man's hand still wrapped around Hope's arm. "Let her go."

The man looked uncertain and loosened his grip. Derrick outweighed him by at least fifty pounds of muscle and could easily take him on if necessary, but he'd prefer to avoid a physical confrontation.

"Joshua is a former employee." Hope yanked her arm from the man's grasp. Her skin was white where his grip had been. She pulled the sleeve of her shirt lower to cover the spot. "He seems to think I owe him something."

"I didn't deserve to be fired for one mistake." Joshua crossed his arms and glared at Hope.

"It wasn't *one* mistake. Do you really want to do this?" Hope asked.

Joshua nodded.

"I kept records. You were late to work every day for a month. On top of that, you didn't show up every Friday. You are lucky I didn't fire you sooner."

He waved a piece of paper that looked like a check. "My paycheck is short."

"No, it's probably too high. When you take company property, it's docked from your pay. That's how it works."

The dude stole from her?

"I didn't take nothin'."

Derrick cringed inside. He was no grammarian, but even he was bothered by Joshua's slaughter of the English language. He took a step closer in case Joshua tried to get physical again with Hope. No way would he lay a finger on her on his watch.

Hope crossed her arms and narrowed her eyes. "I have a witness. Now you can either leave quietly, or I'll press charges and have you arrested for theft and assault."

Based on the track marks on his arm, the police would also find drugs in his possession.

"You're gonna regret this!" Joshua cursed and stormed from the room.

Hope let out a long breath. "Thanks. If you hadn't come along when you did . . ." All her bravado deflated, and her shoulders slumped. "I know how to take care of myself, but I'm so glad I didn't have to hurt him."

He doubted she could have inflicted any harm on the man. "Speaking of being hurt. Are you all right?"

She held up her arm, which shook. "I'll have a bruise, but I'm okay."

"Good. Because if he had hurt you . . ." He didn't know what he'd have done and was thankful he wouldn't need to find out.

Hope still trembled. He reached out and rested a hand on her shoulder. "Do you have to deal with that kind of thing often?"

"Thankfully, no."

Relief shot through him, and he pulled her into a

hug. He suddenly realized his heart was pounding uncharacteristically hard and quickly ended the hug. When had he come to care so much for this woman? They barely knew each other, yet he was drawn to her in a way he didn't expect he'd ever feel again. He strode to the balcony sliding door to check the lock. "How'd he get in here anyway?"

"I was missing a tool today when I was working out at the cabins and thought I may have left it in here. I'd propped the door open while I was looking for it. When I came out of the restroom he was standing there. He had closed the door." She shuddered. "I should go."

"Gabe is coming over for dinner and a movie tonight. How about you join us? After all, inviting him over was your idea." He grinned, hoping to help her relax and put what happened behind her. "Jill is helping Alyssa make the meal. I'm sure there's plenty for all of us."

"Will your sister be there too?"

He shrugged and made his way back to her side. "It's hard to say. Sometimes she sticks around to eat, and other times she doesn't. What do you say?"

"I don't know."

"You should be with friends tonight. Not holed up in your room at the B&B." Besides he was afraid Joshua might try something, and he'd feel better if she was with him.

"Spending the evening someplace other than my room does sound nice," she murmured, seeming to be deep in thought. Her face cleared, and she met his gaze. "Why *are* you here anyway?"

His neck heated. "I stopped in to make sure everything looked okay."

"Good. I'll need you to sign off on the work we did anyway, but I don't have the contract with me at the moment."

He nodded once. "Tell you what. I'll look at the work later. We're already late. Alyssa is probably wondering where I am." He could come in early Monday morning to check on things. Or maybe he'd do it tomorrow since he had to put in a few hours in the afternoon.

Her face relaxed. "That sounds good. I need to stop by the kitchen first and tell Zoe I won't need dinner tonight."

"Assuming she's already boxed it up, she can't sell it now. Why not take the meal and save it for tomorrow?"

"Great idea."

He held the door for Hope and walked her to the kitchen, then to her car. "Follow me." He'd driven his SUV rather than his motorcycle since there'd been a chance of rain in the forecast.

A short time later, they pulled into his driveway. It looked like Jill had already left. He slid out and waited for Hope.

She held up the bag as she approached. "Mind if I stash this in your fridge?"

"Not at all." He led the way inside. "I'm home," he called out.

"Finally! You're late," Alyssa said from the kitchen. "Gabe will be here any minute. I need help setting the table." She walked into the entry. Her face brightened.

"Oh! Hi, Hope. I didn't know you were coming."

She raised the bag. "I have my own food, if there's not enough."

Alyssa giggled. "I made spaghetti. There's more than enough. Come with me."

It looked like things were getting off to a great start. He went to his room and quickly changed into jeans, forgoing his usual sweatshirt for a casual button up. The doorbell resonated through the house. "I'll get it." He rushed out and toward the entryway, but Alyssa had beaten him there.

Gabe stepped inside and placed a kiss on her cheek. "Hi, beautiful," he said softly.

Alyssa's face turned bright pink. Derrick's stomach knotted at Gabe's show of affection, but then he noticed Alyssa's pink face and relaxed. He wanted to be angry at the clean cut young man, but his daughter's obvious embarrassment was too funny—it was only a peck on the cheek. He laughed, but turned it into a cough when Hope stepped into view and gave him a warning look. He held his hand out to the young man. "I'm Derrick, Alyssa's dad, and this is our friend Hope."

Gabe gripped his hand firmly. "It's nice to meet you sir, and you too, Hope." He released Derrick's hand and sniffed the air. "Smells like spaghetti sauce."

"Uh-huh," Alyssa said. A dreamy look covered her face.

Oh boy. His daughter had it bad for this guy. "How about we move this party to the kitchen. I'm starving."

That seemed to draw Alyssa from her trance. "Right.

I have bread in the oven."

They moseyed into the kitchen and sat at the round table. A huge bowl of spaghetti with meat sauce rested in the center along with a green salad and dressing. Alyssa placed a basket with a loaf of bread wrapped inside a towel on the table. Dinner passed uneventfully, and they soon moved into the family room to watch the original *Star Wars* movie.

Alyssa plopped onto the loveseat, and after one look in Derrick's direction, Gabe sat on the floor beneath where he could have sat. He appreciated the gesture. Gabe had been respectful through dinner and had even cleared his own plate. Something Derrick often forgot to do.

"I've seen this movie a dozen times," Derrick said. "I'll do dishes tonight."

"I'll help." Hope popped up from the easy chair she'd sat in.

"That's okay."

"I insist." She gave him a look he suspected meant don't argue. She followed him into the kitchen and pushed up her sleeves. The spot on her arm where Joshua had held her already showed a bruise. "I'll wash, and you can dry since you know where everything goes."

"Or I can rinse and you can load the dishwasher."

She chuckled. "Deal." She leaned in close. "Good call on the dishes. It shows you trust them."

"Thanks. I wasn't thinking of that, but now that you mention it, Gabe seems like a nice guy. I didn't want to like him, but I see why she does." At about five foot nine the kid had an all American boy look. Derrick flipped up the faucet lever. "You want to talk about earlier?"

"Not particularly."

Too bad. He'd tried not to let on how bothered he was by her former employee, but he was concerned for her safety. What if that dude came around when no one was there to stop him from doing whatever he wanted? "Do you think he's dangerous?"

"It's possible. I noticed track marks on his arms. I suspected he might be using, but until this evening when he got in my space, I didn't know for sure."

"You don't require drug tests for your employees?"

"I do before they start on the job, but that's it. I may need to change that policy. I have my crews divided into two-man teams for jobs like this and never worked directly with him, so I didn't know."

Derrick frowned. It'd be hard to make sure she was safe now that she was working at the cabins rather than inside the resort hotel.

"What'cha thinking?"

"Nothing." He didn't care to annoy her by being overly protective. She looked like she could handle herself, but if he hadn't walked in when he had . . .

"You're worried."

He stopped rinsing dishes and looked at her. "What?" How could she possibly know that?

She shrugged. "The question is, are you worried about me or your daughter? Considering Gabe appears to be a gentleman, I'm guessing it's me. But you don't need to worry about me. I can take care of myself."

He shut off the water, glanced toward the family room and drew her into his office, a small room off the kitchen, and closed the door. "You said yourself if I hadn't come in when I did . . ."

"I would have taken him down, and probably injured him. I didn't want to do that."

He laughed. "Seriously? You're fit, but I don't think you could have defended yourself against a physical attack."

With the speed of a viper, she grasped his arm and twisted it behind his back then knocked him to the floor landing a knee into his back. He winced. "What was that?" Pain sliced through his arm and back.

"That was a demonstration." She stood and offered him a hand up.

He waved it off. "No thanks." Although impressed, he was angry that she felt the need to demonstrate on him. He stood. "Where'd you learn to do that?"

"My dad's a cop. He taught me to defend myself. I've never actually had to use my knowledge on a threat, but it's good to know I have the skills should the need arise."

"Did he also teach you to attack unsuspecting innocent men?" He tried to lighten his tone but heard the undertone of anger in his voice.

"No. Sorry about that. I didn't hurt you, did I?" Concern clouded her eyes. She reached a hand toward him, but this time he was too quick and moved away.

He strode toward the door. "I think we should call it

a night. Thanks for your help with the dishes." Okay, so maybe his male pride was a bit wounded.

"Please don't be angry, Derrick."

"It's fine." Though he said the words, even to his own ears they didn't ring true.

She pulled open the door and marched ahead of him. Retrieving her belongings, including her bagged dinner from the fridge, she waved to the kids. "I'm heading out. It was nice meeting you, Gabe."

Alyssa paused the movie and stood. "Why are you leaving?" She walked over to them.

"It's time."

Alyssa narrowed her eyes. "What did you do, Dad?"

Hope chuckled. "He didn't do anything. I did. Good night, Alyssa." She pulled open the door and stepped into the darkness, lit only by the porch light.

Alyssa crossed her arms and tapped her foot. "What was that, Dad?"

"Nothing you need to worry about. How's the movie?"

"Great." She frowned and lowered her voice. "You don't have to tell me what happened, but I hope you fix it. I like Hope. She's good for you, and I can tell you like her too." She spun around, returned to the family room, and plopped back onto the loveseat.

How did he become the bad guy? And what did she mean by Hope was good for him?

A couple of hours later, he stood barely out of view as Gabe said goodbye to his daughter.

"Your dad is cool, Alyssa. Thanks for having me

over."

"Really? You think he's cool?"

"Yes, and we don't have to leave the island to go on a date if it bothers him that much. Maybe we can go kayaking or paddle boarding this weekend instead."

"I'd like to paddle board."

Derrick cleared his throat and moved into view of the teens. "Taking off, Gabe?"

"Yes, sir. Would it be okay if Alyssa and I go paddle boarding tomorrow afternoon?"

"Sure. But don't fall in. The water's still pretty cold."

Alyssa shot him a look that clearly stated "duh."

He thrust out his hand toward Gabe. "It was nice having you here this evening. You're welcome to come over anytime I'm home." He liked the kid but wanted to set boundaries.

"Thanks. See you tomorrow, Alyssa." He turned and left.

Alyssa closed the door, locked it, then turned slowly and did a happy dance. "I get to date Gabe." She threw her arms around his waist. "Thanks, Daddy."

His heart melted as he hugged her back. He hadn't really thought about paddle boarding being a date, but she was right, she'd won. "You're welcome. We'll discuss the rules tomorrow."

Her arms dropped, and she looked up at him with a scowl. "Rules?"

He nodded.

"Fine. Now will you tell me what's up with you and Hope? She seemed off when she left."

His gut tightened as the humiliating event played out in his mind again. "Nothing. She demonstrated some self-defense skills on me to prove she can take care of herself. A man was bothering her at work, and I stepped in."

"Oh. Did you get mad at her or something?"

His face warmed. "I'd rather not discuss it anymore." He yawned. "Time for bed. See you in the morning."

"Are you working tomorrow?"

"Only in the afternoon."

"But I have a date."

He grinned. "I didn't realize I was invited." He pulled out his phone. "In that case, let me call Piper and see if she can fill in for a few hours."

Alyssa grabbed his arm. "No! You can't do that."

He chuckled. "I was teasing. But seriously, why do you need me to be home?"

She shrugged. "I don't know. I just thought you would be."

Hmm. Seemed his daughter might be feeling a little insecure. "How about you come to work with me, and you can paddle board in the lake at the resort."

Her eyes lit. "That could work. I'll text Gabe before I go to sleep and suggest meeting him there. Thanks, Dad."

"You're welcome." He moved down the hall.

"Hey, Dad."

"Yep."

"It's okay with me if you want to date Hope." She stepped into her room and closed the door.

He stood immobilized in the hallway. *Date Hope?*

CHAPTER SEVEN

HOPE SAT AT THE GRANITE-TOPPED island in the B&B, her hands wrapped around a mug of hot chocolate. After leaving Derrick's place she'd driven around the island until she ran out of places to drive and finally came back to the B&B.

Jill sat to her right and Zoe to her left. When Jill saw her walk in, she dragged her to the kitchen demanding to know what was wrong, and they'd been there ever since. It was after eleven PM, and they should be getting their beauty sleep. Hope was on her second cup of hot cocoa and still hadn't spoken. What was she supposed to say to Derrick's sister, or Zoe for that matter? It's not like they were close friends she shared personal stuff with.

Zoe shifted in her seat. "There's something about living on a small island. We all seem to get into one another's business sooner or later." She chuckled softly. "You don't have to tell us what has that storm brewing inside you, but please know we're here if you ever feel like using one of us as a sounding board."

Suddenly clarity hit, and Hope knew what to say. She cleared her throat. "Thanks, Zoe. I appreciate that." She glanced at Jill. "You're probably going to hear about this sooner or later, so I might as well be the one to tell you. I went to dinner tonight at your brother's place."

"I know. He called after you left."

Figures. "I don't care to go into details, but to prove a point I used some self-defense moves on him, and I think I wounded his pride. End of story."

Jill's eyes widened. "Why would you do that? Did he . . . no. He'd never. He's a prince among men."

"I don't know about the prince part, but no, he didn't do anything except show concern for a situation I'm dealing with. I don't know why I felt a demonstration would be better than telling him about my training."

Zoe chuckled. "Seems to me he got the point."

Hope couldn't help smiling. "True, but now I feel bad, and he's kind of angry with me."

"He'll get over it. My brother is not one to hold a grudge." Jill's eyes gleamed with mischief.

"What's going on in that head of yours? You look like you're up to something." Hope didn't think the stuffy B&B manager capable of mischief, but she'd seen that look plenty of times in her life and it always meant trouble. Maybe she'd misjudged Jill.

"I'm not up to anything, but it's going to be so much fun teasing my brother."

"No! You can't say anything until he tells you. I don't want him to think I'm a gossip." She looked Jill in the eyes. "Promise me you won't say anything."

The mirth on Jill's face evaporated. "Okay, if it means that much to you."

"It does. Thank you."

Zoe yawned and stood. "I'm sorry, ladies, but I need to sleep. My alarm goes off at five. I'm beat."

Hope's heart warmed toward Zoe. "Thanks for caring enough to lose sleep for me."

"You'll have to teach me a few of your moves someday. You never know when they'll come in handy."

"Me too," Jill said.

"Deal." Hope grinned and placed her mug in the sink.

"Will you still be here for Easter at the end of the month, Hope?" Zoe asked.

"Probably. Why?"

"Nick and I are hosting a big meal on Easter after church. You're invited."

"Thanks!" At least one good thing came of this night. "I'd love to come. Should I bring something?"

"Rachel and her family will be here, so maybe some earplugs." She chuckled. "Between her five-year-old son and the baby, and all the other guests, I expect things to get a little wild here on Easter. You can help hide plastic eggs in the yard if you'd like."

"That sounds like a lot of fun. I'd love to help any way I can. I should head to bed too. Good night." Hope pushed open the swinging door and walked through the dining room which led to the entryway and the staircase to the second-floor bedrooms.

At first she'd been angry at Derrick's reaction, then she only felt guilt. She probably owed him an apology, but she was afraid he'd want nothing to do with her. And that hurt more than she expected. She liked him—a lot. Sure, he irritated her at times, and he wasn't her type, at least on the surface. But as Piper had pointed out in her own special way, Hope's type hadn't worked out thus far—especially her last relationship. Was it too late to repair the damage with Derrick?

Saturday morning, Hope looked out her bedroom window and made a decision to go exploring just as soon as she stopped in to check on Piper. Other than driving around last night in the dark, she had taken no time to acquaint herself with her temporary home. She hoped to convince Piper to be her tour guide.

Hope showered then dressed and decided to opt for short sleeves since it looked so nice outside. She trotted down the stairs and pulled up short before hitting the landing at the bottom. Her heart rate kicked into double time. "Derrick. What are you doing here?" He wore a leather jacket and jeans. Maybe he was more her type than she'd realized. It should be a crime for a man to look that good.

"I had to drop off Alyssa, and I wanted to talk to you, so I've been waiting."

"Oh." She walked down the remaining stairs and shot a look to her right toward the dining room. "I need coffee. Be right with you." She grabbed a disposable cup and filled it almost to the top, added half and half and a smidge of sugar, then popped on a lid, took a muffin from a basket and headed back to him.

"That's your breakfast?"

"I slept in and missed the meal. This will be fine." She took a long draw from the cup willing the caffeine to kick in. Somehow being around Derrick turned her brain to a puddle of mush—not good.

"What are your plans for the day?"

"I thought I'd drag Piper from her bed and let her play tour guide."

He frowned. "Are you sure that's a good idea? I mean, she's supposed to be on bed rest. My wife had to go on bed rest when she was pregnant with Alyssa, and she wasn't supposed to be active."

Hope frowned. "I didn't realize it was such a strict thing, or that sitting in the car would be considered active. Okay then, I guess I'm on my own."

"Not necessarily. Alyssa is in my sister's suite. It's Jill's day off, and they're going shopping this morning. You could join them."

She wrinkled her nose. "Nothing against your sister or daughter, but shopping isn't my favorite pastime."

"Seriously? I thought all women liked shopping."

"Nope. In case you haven't noticed, I'm not exactly a stereotypical woman."

He chuckled. "Point taken. I rode, but I have an extra helmet. I could give you a tour. I don't need to be at work until this afternoon."

Her stomach fluttered at the idea of riding on the

back of his Indian Chief Classic. She'd always loved that bike. Would being so close to him be awkward after last night? She still needed to apologize. Then again she couldn't pass up an opportunity like this. "So you're not mad at me anymore?"

"Nope. But no more demonstrations, please." One corner of his mouth tipped up.

"I promise."

Derrick's cell phone rang. He looked at the caller ID and quickly answered. Not wanting to eavesdrop, Hope wandered into the sitting room, sat at the piano and plucked out the Jeopardy song.

"There's a problem at the resort. I'm sorry, but I'm not going to be able to give you that tour after all. I need to head over there right now."

She forced a smile. "No problem. I can entertain myself." In fact, maybe rather than touring the island she'd head home for the day. Her house in Tacoma was only an hour away. It wasn't like she had to spend her weekends here too. If she hurried she'd make the next ferry. "See you Monday." She took the stairs two at a time. It would be wonderful to sleep in her own bed tonight. She'd give her parents a quick call, alerting them that she was heading to her place for the weekend since her dad took care of it when she was away.

Thirty minutes later, she waited in line for the ferry. Ominous looking clouds rolled by overhead. Maybe they'd get some much-needed rain. Unease coursed through her. What was up with that? Rain was a good thing. The ferry approached and was within minutes of docking. Her stomach knotted so tight, she almost doubled over. She'd felt fine earlier. What was going on? One thing was certain, she wouldn't be going home today.

Derrick looked up from the computer screen at the front lobby counter and moved his neck side to side. After dealing with the problem this morning, he'd decided to stick around. The morning flew by, and he only had a few more hours until his shift was over.

"Hi, Dad." Alyssa walked up to the counter wearing cutoff jeans and a black tank top.

"Hey pumpkin. What's up? Did you need something?" *Like a jacket?* The last time he'd looked it was overcast and cool. She was going to catch a cold dressed like that. She sure hadn't been wearing that earlier when he'd dropped her off at the B&B.

"You said you'd hook us up with paddle boards."

"That's right." He opened a drawer, pulled out two passes, and slid them across the counter. "What happened to the sweats you had on earlier?"

She patted her oversized purse draped across her body. "They're in here. The sun is finally shining, and it's nice out. I want to work on a tan."

"Oh. I hope you're wearing sunblock." He'd been so busy, he hadn't noticed it was brighter outside now than when he'd arrived.

She rolled her eyes.

There was no point in making a scene, so he'd drop the matter. "Is Gabe here yet?"

"No. He had to help his mom with something, but he won't be long." Her eyes widened. "Did you hear about Hope?"

A jolt shot through him. "What about her?" He tried to sound casual, but something about the tone in his daughter's voice told him something was up.

"She was going to spend the weekend at her house, but when she went to board the ferry, she felt terrible. Aunt Jill and I saw her as she was heading to her room."

"She's sick?"

"I guess so. We only stayed long enough for a quick lunch then Aunt Jill brought me here."

"No one checked on her?" It wasn't like his nosey sister not to know everything about everyone in the B&B. "Maybe I should call her and see how she's doing."

"You have her number?" Surprise lit his daughter's voice. She rested her elbows on the countertop. "Have you asked her out yet?"

"What is it with you lately? Because you have a boyfriend, it doesn't mean the rest of us need to be in a relationship." Although, the more he thought about Hope, the more the idea appealed. He liked that she could take care of herself if she needed to, that she was an independent thinker, a hard worker, smart, and that she was a genuinely nice person.

"Testy. Testy." She backed away from the counter with a grin on her face.

"Whatever." His daughter's vernacular had rubbed off on him.

She giggled. "Thanks for the passes."

"You're welcome. Will you need a ride home?"

"Maybe. I'll text you."

He nodded and pulled his phone from his pocket. His thumb poised over the keypad. Hope was an independent woman who could take care of herself, but even an independent woman needed concerned friends.

I hear you aren't feeling well. Do you need anything? He pressed send and waited. A moment later his phone chimed announcing a new text message.

Feeling better. Does the restaurant make chicken soup?

He dialed the kitchen and spoke with Rachel. As it turned out chicken and vegetable soup was on the lunch menu. He ordered some to go, then texted. *Yes. Will drop some by soon.*

Thanks!

Thirty minutes later, he stood outside Hope's bedroom door at the B&B and knocked.

She pulled the door open. "Oh. I thought you'd text when you got here."

"I wasn't sure if you were up to coming downstairs." He held out the bag as he checked her over from head to toe. She'd changed since this morning and now wore black sweats and a hoodie. She looked as cuddly as a teddy bear. It took all his willpower to refrain from finding out if she was as cuddly as she looked.

Her hair fell softly around her pale face making him

want to reach out and touch it. He shook the thought from his mind and focused on why he was here. To deliver food and make sure the lead electrician for the resort was okay. "You look better than I expected."

Hope grasped the bag. "Thanks. I'm feeling a lot better. I don't know what came over me, but I didn't want to risk a heavy meal in case I have a stomach bug."

"On that note, I should go."

She chuckled. "Afraid you'll get sick?"

"No." He'd wanted to see with his own eyes that she was okay, and other than looking pale, she seemed fine. "I need to return to work. Alyssa might want a ride home after her date, and I promised I'd be there."

She nodded. "Your daughter is so cute. How are things going with her now that you had Gabe over and allowed their date today?"

"Better." At least, mostly better. He had a feeling things were not as perfect as they seemed, but maybe that was the pessimist in him.

She nodded and stepped back. "I owe you for this."

"Don't worry about it. Consider it a peace offering." He winked.

She gave a half-smile and closed the door.

He stood there a moment longer. Had he said something wrong?

Hope's heart pounded as she stood on the other side of her bedroom door listening for Derrick to walk away. She hadn't expected him to have a sense of humor regarding what had happened between them.

She didn't want to like the man, but he was hard not to like, and the more she got to know him the more she had to acknowledge that Piper's matchmaking skills were on target. But did she want to see where things led with Derrick? They were clearly on their way to being friends, but she would be leaving the island soon and wasn't willing to do the long distance thing. Not that an hour's drive was that far, but it would be difficult for them to connect with the demands on both of their lives.

She sighed and moved to the table and chair beside the window that looked onto the Puget Sound, then pulled out the meal Derrick had delivered. She carefully pried the lid off the soup and breathed deeply of the comforting scent. *Mmm.*

Her cell phone rang the melody assigned to her dad's phone. Though tempted to ignore it, she swiped the screen. "Hi, Dad. What's up?"

"Thank God."

"Excuse me?" Her dad never spoke like that unless he really meant it. "Why are we thanking God?"

"You're alive." His voice caught, and she could hear him sobbing in the distance as if he'd put the phone down.

CHAPTER EIGHT

HOPE SAT UP STRAIGHT. HER HEART jolted. "Dad! What's wrong?" She tried to get his attention several more times, practically shouting into the phone. She'd never heard him sob like this. Had never even seen him cry. Talk about feeling helpless. "Dad!" Tears pricked her eyes. At this rate another guest in the B&B would turn her into Jill for making too much noise.

He gradually quieted then blew his nose. "I'm sorry." He cleared his throat. "We thought." He cleared his throat again. "Your mom and I thought you were inside your house."

My house? "What's going on?"

He took a loud deep breath and let it out slowly. "Did you come home like you said you were going to?"

"No. I started feeling bad while in line for the ferry and decided to stay on the island. I'm sorry for not calling. Is that what this is about? Were you waiting at my house for me all this time?"

"No. I hate to be the bearer of bad news, but I'm so thankful you're alive to tell it to."

Her stomach knotted again. This did not sound good.

"We had some weather here today."

"It rained?" That's great news. Why would rain upset her dad? They'd been in the midst of a drought and everything was bone dry.

"Yes, it rained some, but mostly we had lightning. It struck the tree in your backyard."

Her stomach sank. "The half-dead, eighty-foot Douglas fir?" She should have hired professionals to remove the dying tree this past fall, but she'd been busy and figured it would be fine until she had time to deal with it.

"Yes. Sweetie. It not only caught fire when the lightning hit, but it crashed on top of your house. Your neighbors were out, and no one saw the fire until it was too late. It's a complete loss." His voice caught again. "We were afraid you'd been trapped inside by the fallen tree and couldn't escape. Your car and motorcycle were in the garage. I had not gone in there since you left, and assumed you were inside."

"I'm sorry for scaring you." A wave of dizziness overcame her. "I'm driving my company SUV." What was she going to do? Other than her metal working tools that she'd loaned to a friend and what she had with her, all her worldly possessions were in that place.

"That's the best news I've heard all day. Things can be replaced, but you can't."

Mom's muffled voice asked for the phone. "Hope?"

"Yes, Mom."

"It's so good to hear your voice. You don't worry

about a thing. Your dad will get the claim going with your insurance."

"Shouldn't I come home and sift through what's left?"

"You could, but from what the firefighters said, there's nothing here that's salvageable. If you really want to come, and I don't blame you if you do, come tomorrow."

"I'll do that." She wanted to go today, but it made sense to wait until tomorrow. The hot spots would be out, and she'd be able to rummage through her house. Maybe she'd find something worth saving.

"I'm so thankful you weren't home. Why'd you change your mind?"

She repeated the story to her mom. It was probably the longest they'd spoken since she'd destroyed her career as a sculptor. Talking with her like this felt natural and odd at the same time. "The weird thing is that once I decided to stay put, I started to feel better, but not well enough to drive for an hour in weekend traffic."

Dad spoke into the extension. "The Lord was watching out for you today."

Awareness settled over her, and tears streamed down her face. He was right. The Lord had protected her today.

Hope sat in the recliner that Chase had brought into Piper's bedroom for visitors and told her friend about her house. After hearing the news, she felt antsy and needed to get out.

"You're sure you're not sick?" Piper eyed her skeptically with her hands resting on her growing midsection.

"Positive. Other than feeling out of sorts, and a little angry, I'm fine."

"What are you angry about?"

"From what my parents said, my house was destroyed."

"Not to sound callous, but you have insurance right?"

Hope nodded.

"Then thank the Lord you weren't there and move on. You can rebuild. You've been saying since you moved into that house that the bathrooms and kitchen needed updating."

"True. But it sounds like I lost everything! I truly believe the Lord stopped me from going home today to protect me, and I'm grateful, but if He can protect me, why didn't He save my house? He could've stopped the lightning from striking the tree."

Piper sighed. "I don't know why God does or doesn't do things. Why can't you just accept what happened and move on?"

"Because that's not how I'm wired," Hope snapped. Her shoulders slumped. "I'm sorry. I shouldn't be taking out my frustrations on you." Piper hadn't had an easy road either. "How do you keep your faith in the Lord when bad things happen?"

"Jeremiah 29:11 is my favorite verse. *For I know the thoughts that I think toward you, says the* LORD, *thoughts of peace and not of evil, to give you a future and a hope.* God is not out to harm his children. He loves us and wants what is best for us."

"So, you're saying losing virtually everything I own is in my best interest?" Hope couldn't see how that was possible.

"Maybe. Look, I'm not going to pretend I know how God operates. You asked a question, and I gave you the first answer that popped into my head. I could be wrong. Maybe you should ask *Him* instead of me. What do I know?"

"Good point." She made a silly face at her friend. "I'm sorry for snapping."

"All is forgiven. Did I ever tell you about the tree that nearly killed me?"

Hope's eyes widened, and she leaned forward. "No. What happened?"

"Chase and I were sitting at a park in his truck here on the island. A major thunderstorm passed overhead. A tree was struck by lightning and crashed down on the cab of the truck. We barely escaped before it hit."

"Were you hurt?"

"A piece of glass hit me, and I needed stitches, but other than being shaken up, we were fine. Chase's truck was another matter. Completely totaled. But he had great insurance and was able to get a truck he liked even better."

"Why didn't you tell me about this?"

"It's not a memory I like to re-live. The point is—yes, it was scary, and yes, it was a pain, but in the end I was fine. Things can be replaced, and your memories are here." She pointed to her head.

"I suppose you're right, but this is going to be a huge time drain. I don't know how I'm going to rebuild and finish the job here. I may need to turn things here over to my foreman."

"No."

Hope's gaze shot to Piper. "Excuse me?"

"Let me help you. I have a ton of contacts and can do everything from the comfort of, or lack thereof," she made a face, "my bed."

"I don't know. This is my problem. I need to deal with it. Besides, you're on bed rest. I don't want you to do anything that will cause stress and harm you or your baby."

Piper scowled. "Don't you think I know my limits? I was in the land development business for years. What you need done is child's play for someone like me. Please let me help. I need *you,* not your foreman. Plus, I'm bored. I can do everything from my laptop and phone. And if there's something that I can't handle I'll let you know."

"Okay. But I'm going to hire Duncan to draw up the design. I want to go with the same general floor plan, but after living in that house for a couple of years, I have some ideas on how to improve the flow."

"Great idea! Duncan is an exceptional architect, and

knowing him, he'll be a local set of eyes to help us out when neither of us can be there."

"True." They'd been friends with Duncan for years, and she knew he'd do an exceptional job easing the burden from both of them once she explained their situation.

"I heard Duncan is single and available again." Piper waggled her brows. "The two of you would make a cute couple."

Been there done that—sort of. "I thought you were rooting for Derrick. And what's this sudden obsession with fixing me up?"

Piper shrugged. "I want to see you happy and settled. It's been a while since you've been either."

Her friend was right, but she wouldn't admit it out loud. Instead she stood and hugged Piper. "You are a troublemaker. Take care. I'll stop in again soon." She left the house and pondered her friend's words. Hope had been the one to break things off with Duncan even though he said he agreed they shouldn't date. Derrick was growing on her and she wasn't the slightest bit interested in Duncan.

Monday morning, Derrick stopped by the cabins to check on the progress of the electrical work. Tradesmen moved in and out of various cabins. He didn't see anyone he recognized, so he went into the first cabin he came to that had no activity around it, anxious to check this off his to-do list. He flipped the light switch—nothing. Odd, he'd been told this cabin was finished.

He pulled out his cell phone and pressed the flashlight app. "Oh, no." His stomach sank. Wires were pulled from the walls and hung haphazardly. Had Hope's unhappy former employee done more than threaten her?

A gasp sounded behind him. He whirled around and shined the light on the person. "Hope." Fear and disbelief covered her face.

"What happened?"

He walked toward the doorway where she still stood. "I'm calling the police. Let's wait outside." He placed the call, then turned to Hope. "I need to check the other cabin you were working on."

Her troubled eyes cleared. "You don't think . . . ." She raced ahead of him and stood motionless in the doorway.

He looked over her shoulder and blew out a slow breath. "How many days will this set us back?"

"I don't know. I'm short a man. There's so much to do. I simply don't know." She turned and brushed past him.

He understood the defeat in her voice, but she seemed even more downtrodden than he'd expect. He found her leaning against the hood of her SUV, her arms crossed and her face stricken. "Hey, it's not that bad if we lose a week or so. Piper will understand." At least he hoped it would only be a week. They were already taking reservations for these cabins and needed them to be completed as close to on time as possible.

"From the brief look I had, we'll need to start from scratch, and it will take time to pull all that wire out." She shook her head. "I can't afford this. Between the deductible on my house and now this . . . I'm ruined." She sighed. "To help keep costs down, I have a huge deductible with my business insurance, too. I don't have enough cash flow right now. I should have walked out of here the first day when Piper tried to play matchmaker with us." She raised her chin. "I actually quit, but she begged me to stay. This is what I get for being a softy."

Piper playing matchmaker? Tingles zipped through him. "What are you talking about?" What had he missed

"Sorry, I figured you'd heard. My house caught fire on Saturday. I went to see it yesterday, and it's a complete loss."

"Oh, man. I'm really sorry to hear about your house, but the resort's insurance will cover the damage here, so you don't need to stress about that." She sure didn't need to deal with this vandalism on top of her house. "Whatever I can do to help, please let me know."

She slid a glance his way. "Unless you're a licensed electrician, I don't know what you can do."

"As it happens, I am."

Her eyes widened. "Have you kept your electrical license up to date?"

He nodded.

"Then I could use some help getting back on schedule."

"I'll do anything I can." He was already working fifty hours a week, but he'd do whatever it took to make sure this project was completed on time.

"Thanks."

"Of course. Now what was that business about a matchmaker?"

"Don't tell me you never figured it out?"

His mind raced to grasp what she was implying.

"Piper wanted you looking over my shoulder so we'd be forced to spend time together." Though her voice was low, frustration shouted loud and clear.

He wasn't in the habit of questioning his boss's orders, but he had thought Piper was being extreme when it came to Hope's work. He winced. *Matchmaker.* "You think she is trying to set *us* up?"

She nodded.

Was everyone plotting his future? First Alyssa and now Piper. He didn't blame Hope one iota for being upset.

A police cruiser pulled up and parked. Derrick would have to think about all of this new information later.

CHAPTER NINE

THE FOLLOWING WEEKEND, AFTER A LONG, hard week, sunshine beat down on Hope as she sat in the backyard of the Wildflower B&B with her gaze focused on the Sound. A sailboat soared in the distance. She'd love to sail away and leave her problems behind, but that wasn't going to happen.

She'd never worked so many hours in a week. Derrick had even helped out each night. He knew what he was doing, needed zero guidance, and he was quick, which really surprised her considering he wasn't a practicing electrician. She leaned her head back and closed her eyes. The insurance money for the vandalism had not come in yet, and she needed to buy replacement supplies. How would she cover the expense?

"Good afternoon, Hope."

She opened an eye and spied Zoe standing in her sunlight.

"Hey there. Have a seat."

"Thanks." Zoe eased into the chair beside her. "I

heard about the rough week you've had. I can't believe someone would not only vandalize the cabins like that, but specifically target the electrical work."

"I agree. At least they know who did it."

Zoe swiveled to face her. "That's news. Who did it?"

"A disgruntled former employee of mine. Thankfully he was arrested. I should have figured he'd pull something after he threatened me, but this is unfamiliar territory for me. I didn't consider what he was capable of."

"I'm glad you don't deal with that kind of thing on a regular basis. I had to let someone go who was stealing from the restaurant about a year ago. Mercifully, she left the island and didn't cause any problems. How are you doing with all that has happened?"

"I'm hanging in there. How about you?"

"I'm fine, but I'm concerned about you. Is there anything I can do to help?"

"Not unless you can loan me some money," she said playfully.

"How much are we talking about?"

Her heart leapt. "Oh no, Zoe! I wasn't serious. I would never take a loan from you. I'm just feeling sorry for myself."

"Do you need a loan?"

"No." In reality she could put everything on her credit card and settle up once Piper paid her.

"Then maybe you'd like to talk. I spend most of my waking hours around people, but I hardly ever get to visit with anyone."

That sounded familiar. "What would you like to talk about?"

"You and this island."

Hope chuckled. "Ok-a-yyy." What could Zoe possibly have to say?

"I heard about your house, and I was thinking how nice it would be to have an electrician on the island fulltime."

"I don't know. That's a big leap for me. On top of that, I'd have to commute every day, and that would be a hassle."

"Not necessarily. There are people moving to the island all the time and most are buying fixer uppers with ancient wiring that needs updating. I can't tell you how many electrical company vans from the mainland I've seen since moving here. Speaking of vehicles, why do you drive an SUV rather than the typical van?"

"I don't like vans." She'd driven a van at one time, but it was too big. She let her crew use that vehicle and purchased an SUV. Considering how much time she usually spent on the road the purchase was essential. "What's going on, Zoe? I know you don't have time for small talk, especially with the Easter preparations."

"Fair enough. I can't explain it without sounding like a religious freak, but I felt the Lord nudging me to come out here and talk with you. Anything in particular we should be talking about?"

Hope tilted her head toward Zoe. She'd been chewing on this since last Saturday. Maybe Zoe would be able to help. "I'm angry with God, and I don't understand what He's doing. Everything keeps going wrong, I feel attacked, and I don't know what to do."

Wide-eyed, Zoe nodded. "Understandable on all accounts. My foster mom always tells me when I don't know what to do, or I'm upset, or pretty much anytime." She chuckled and a soft smile covered her face. "She *always* tells me to pray. Ask the Lord your questions and then wait for an answer. I'm convinced the Lord allows some stuff to happen simply to get our attention. Have you prayed about it?"

Hope stifled a sigh. "You might be right." It wasn't like she didn't pray. She did, but generally for others. She never considered asking Him about her situation and what to do. Or that He might be trying to get her attention. "I believe in the power of prayer, but do you really think prayer will make everything better?" She looked skeptically at Zoe.

"It's possible. I find when something is too big for me, turning it over to Him helps. He doesn't remove the struggles from my life, but He does help me deal with the stuff I allow Him to."

"Hmm. I hadn't thought of it like that. So what you're saying is, if I hold onto a problem the Lord can't help me?" That made perfect sense. Too bad she hadn't thought of it sooner.

"I guess that's the gist of it." Zoe pushed up from the seat beside her. "I could sit out here all afternoon, but I shouldn't. I was serious about you living on the island. I hope you'll at least consider it."

"Thanks, Zoe." Hope reached out and gave her hand

a gentle squeeze. Zoe strolled back inside leaving Hope to ponder their conversation. She stood then wandered down to the beach. Water lapped at the shoreline. *Lord what should I do? How do I get out of this mess and come out unscathed?*

Up ahead she spotted a man and a girl tossing a Frisbee. They resembled Derrick and Alyssa, but in all her jaunts down here, she'd never seen them on the beach together.

Laughter from the pair carried on the breeze and a longing in the pit of her stomach drew her toward the duo. She wanted to be a wife and mother someday, but the older she grew, the more it seemed like an impossible dream.

The man turned and waved.

"Derrick." She said more to herself than him. She picked up the pace and drew near to them. "Hey there."

"Hi, Hope," Alyssa said. "Would you like to play too?"

"Sure." Hope positioned herself so they formed a triangle. The hot pink Frisbee soared toward her, then a gust of wind sent it upward. She jumped high and snagged it then flicked it to Alyssa who then flipped it to her dad, but it veered in Hope's direction. She ran for it and reached it at the same moment as Derrick. Somehow their bodies became entangled, and they both went down.

Silence. His surprised brown eyes with gold flecks looked down at her. She laughed and pushed at his chest. "You caught me, but weren't you supposed to catch the flying disk?"

He pushed up and sat beside her facing the water. "Sorry about that."

Alyssa plopped down on her other side. "You okay?"

"Sure. I had that coming. I should have called it." She glanced toward Derrick. "How about you? Anything broken?"

"I'm intact."

She couldn't help but admire his strong chin and shoulders. Though she'd never seen him work out, he must do so to maintain his physique.

Alyssa stood. "If you two are okay, I'm going to head back to the B&B."

Derrick nodded.

"You're going to be at the B&B for a while?" Hope asked.

"Yes." Alyssa pulled on her hoodie and zipped it up.

"Good. I have a surprise for you."

Her face lit. "Really? What is it?"

Hope pressed her lips together and mimed locking them and tossing the key.

Alyssa shook her head and crossed her arms as if she were disgusted, but Hope could tell from the twinkle in her eyes that she was only playing. "I'll be in the kitchen when you get back. Zoe is giving me a cooking lesson. It's a project for my cooking class at school. Gabe is going to film it."

"Sounds like fun. I'll find you when I get back." She waved as the teen jogged away. She should probably warn Derrick about the surprise she had for his daughter, then thought better of it. Seeing the look on his face would be worth every penny she'd spent.

Derrick rested his hand over hers. "I'm surprised to see you."

"Funny, I felt the same way when I spotted you and Alyssa. How are things going on that front?"

"Better. We have our moments, but your advice was sound. Thanks."

She grinned. "You're welcome." Her heart kicked into double time. She felt like a teen herself when Derrick held her hand. Such a simple gesture turned her insides into a puddle. She chuckled.

"What's so funny?"

"Just thinking."

He raised a brow. "Care to share?"

"Nope." She pressed her lips together.

"Okay." He drew the word out. "What's your surprise for Alyssa?"

"Can't tell."

He released her hand. "I suppose I'll have to get it out of you another way." He suddenly stood then scooped her into his arms.

Tingles shot through her, and she couldn't help laughing. "If you think that will get me to share my secret you're mistaken." She wrapped an arm around his neck hoping to send the message that he wasn't getting her to talk. "This is kind of nice."

He grinned. "Not talking, huh?" He walked, carrying her toward the Sound.

Her eyes widened when she realized what he was up to. She pushed at his chest. "Don't you dare!"

"You ready to talk?"

"No."

Merriment lit his face. "Well then . . ." He stood at the water's edge and turned sideways as if to fling her into the water.

"Okay. I give. Put me down."

"Smart lady." He released her legs, but still held his arm loosely around her waist. "Well?" He brushed a strand of hair away from her face. His eyes probed.

She licked her lips wishing he'd kiss her, but she was too shy to kiss him first. "We should probably—"

He lowered his mouth and his lips melted into hers.

She wrapped both arms around his neck and drew him closer. A sigh of contentment escaped her as he stepped back and brushed his hand through her hair.

"Should I apologize?" Uncertainty filled his eyes.

"You'd better not! If I didn't want you to kiss me, I'd have stopped you." She'd grown to care for Derrick and wished he'd kiss her again.

Humor sparkled in his eyes. "Good to know." He lowered his head and his warm lips found hers again. He pulled her close as she laced her fingers behind his neck. Too soon the kiss ended, but he still held her close. "When I first met you, I sure didn't expect this."

She grinned. "That makes two of us. You're not my type."

He raised a brow. "You have a type?"

"Well, yeah, but my type never works out, so maybe venturing outside my box is a good thing."

He nodded. "I'm not sure I have a type, but if I did,

you wouldn't be it."

She playfully smacked his shoulder and pulled out of his embrace. "Thanks a lot."

He took her hand. "I'm messing with you. So what's that surprise you were about to tell me?"

"What are you talking about? Oh!" No way was she going to tell him before she surprised his daughter. "You're going to have to wait. I only said I'd tell you to get you to put me down."

He waggled his brows. "I have my ways of getting it out of you."

She laughed then slid her hand from his grip, whirled and sprinted in the direction she'd come. Footfalls sounded close behind her. She pushed harder and raced all the way to the backyard of the B&B. Her lungs burned, and her calves cramped. She stopped and paced slowly with hands on her hips trying to catch her breath. Sprinting was not her thing.

Derrick sprawled out on the lawn face down. Apparently sprinting wasn't his thing either. "Remind me never to trust you again."

Hope couldn't help grinning. "You can trust me, Derrick, but when it comes to surprises, don't even ask because I'm not telling."

"Whatever you say." He rolled over and sat up then wiped his forehead on his arm. "I noticed the electrical work in the cabins is back on schedule. I'm impressed."

She stood a little taller. "We couldn't have done it without your help. Thanks for pitching in this past week."

"It was actually kind of fun." He picked a blade of grass. "It's been a while since I enjoyed electrical work. And to think it was once the only thing I wanted to do."

"Sounds familiar. I used to have a side job that was my passion but ended up sticking with electrical work and dropping it." She eased down beside him.

"Seriously? What was it?"

Her gaze skittered to his and stopped. "Can you keep a secret?" She knew he could but needed him to understand this was between them. They'd spent several hours working side-by-side this past week, and he was not one to gossip.

He nodded.

"I am, or was a metal sculpture artist. I was pretty well known and managed to make a decent living at it. Actually my earnings are all tucked away to provide for my retirement someday, since I nearly had two full time jobs."

"Wow. Why'd you quit? Burnout?"

She looked down then back at him, unsure how much to share. But if he was going to be a part of her life, like she suspected, he needed to know what he was getting himself into. "My mom was my manager. She, for reasons still unknown, thought it was okay to take more money than her commission, and on top of that, she spread lies about me to the media with the hope of getting more sales. As if I could handle more than I was already doing." Sadly, her mother was of the school of thought that believed tortured artists garnered more attention and thereby more sales.

"Whoa! That is not what I expected to hear. That was pretty gutsy considering she's married to a cop."

"Dad never knew, and I decided for the sake of their marriage, I wouldn't tell him. Being in law enforcement is hard enough on a marriage. They didn't need that to deal with too."

"So you didn't press charges?"

"No. I was her only client, so it wasn't necessary to protect anyone else from her or drag our family through that."

Awe shone in his eyes. "You are a good daughter. How are you and your mom now?"

"We're civil. I try to be polite, but it's always going to come between us. I trusted her. It hurt more than I thought possible to be betrayed by her."

"I didn't think you were close to your parents based on what you'd told me about them."

"Once I grew up, our relationship improved, then my art started selling well, and I needed help managing the business side of things."

"But you have a degree in business."

She shrugged. "I could only do so much. At the time I was working for another company full time as an electrician and spent all my off hours creating art. I went to art fairs, and soon a few galleries wanted my stuff. It took off, but I couldn't deal with the business side too. My mom had good business sense, or so I thought, so I hired her."

He reached over and grasped her hand. "I'm sorry about what she did to you. But why didn't you fire her and hire someone else? Why give it up?"

"I did fire her. As far as continuing to sculpt, I couldn't. I lost my desire to create art. My ideas used to beg to come out. So much so, I'd often get up in the middle of the night and pencil out drawings of ideas. Now I've got nothing. No inspiration."

He released her hand and tugged her into a side hug. "I'm sorry you were hurt so badly you lost your passion." His voice filled with empathy. "That must have been devastating."

She nodded.

"I'll pray for you to find inspiration again. No one should give up something they care so much about because of someone else's mistakes." He placed a soft kiss on the side of her head.

"Thanks, Derrick. That means a lot." Her heart pitter-pattered. She was falling for him. Big time. After holding people at arm's length for so long, his compassion almost overwhelmed her. Time to make a run for it before she blubbered. "I want to see Alyssa before she leaves, so I'll catch you later. Okay?"

"Sure thing. But, can we get together soon? Maybe we can go paddle boating."

"I'd like that." Warmth filled her heart as she strode toward the bed-and-breakfast in search of Alyssa. Now more than ever, she couldn't wait to give her the surprise. Derrick was sure to be pleased too.

Late that same afternoon Derrick walked into his kitchen, determined to tell Alyssa that he planned to date Hope. Sure, she'd given her blessing, but now that it was really happening, he wanted her to know in case she had any concerns.

Alyssa sat at the kitchen table with her sleeves pushed up, staring at her forearms. She looked at him wearing a huge smile. "Look!" She raised an arm. "Don't you love it? Hope is the coolest! I can't believe she did this for me."

A brownish-colored tattoo cluttered her arm. How and when did Hope have time to do this? Derrick's gut twisted. He fisted his hands by his side and counted to ten.

Hope had assured him it was against the law to tattoo a minor. But if that were the case how did his daughter manage this?

"Isn't it great? I got this one too." Alyssa held out her other arm.

Time seemed to stop as he stared at the heart tattoo with Gabe's name inside. His brain finally unscrambled. "It's something all right. Hope did this to you?"

"Yes. It was her surprise."

No wonder she refused to tell him. She *knew* how he felt yet she went behind his back and did this? Rage burned through him. "I'll be back." He grabbed his keys and stormed out of the house. Hope had some explaining to do. He slipped on his helmet, mounted his bike, and took off.

Overcome with the feeling he needed to stop and think before he confronted Hope, he pulled over and sat there. A light breeze rustled the leaves on nearby maple trees. He killed the engine and paced. Showing up at the B&B furious would not serve anyone well. He liked Hope—a lot, although he was angrier with her than he'd ever been with anyone.

He'd finally convinced some of the busybody women in town that he could do a good job raising his daughter alone and that they didn't need to keep interfering, and now this. All the gossip and dirty looks would start up again. He could handle those women, even if he didn't care to, but what about his daughter? She didn't need to be exposed to their ignorance. When Alyssa was younger she had no idea what people were saying, but she'd surely hear the gossip now.

Lord, please help me to calm down and not say or do anything I'll regret. He did not anger easily, except when it came to someone messing with his family. Didn't Hope understand how dangerous what she did was? What if Alyssa got an infection? Then again, how did Hope get her hands on the equipment? Sure she was an artist, but wouldn't she have to be licensed or certified or whatever it was called? Maybe the tattoo wasn't real. That had to be it, but Hope should at least have talked to him before inking up his daughter's arms. Alyssa could have an allergic reaction and then what?

Or even worse, Hope could have bought a low quality or bad batch of ink. He'd recently seen an article about that happening, and several teens had ended up with serious infections. If he remembered straight, the kids would probably be scarred too because of it. What if that happened to Alyssa?

Lord, please help me here. I'm so angry. I know I need to calm down. Please give me Your peace that passes all understanding.

A few minutes later he calmed, and he felt comfortable confronting Hope now. At least he could speak without losing it.

A short time later, he pulled up to Wildflower B&B. The door swung open and Hope stepped out. Her face lit in surprise. She strode over to him. "Hi there. Long time no see."

He pulled off his helmet. "You're just the person I need to talk to."

She shot him an eager smile. "What'd you think? They turned out great, right? I tried to talk her out of the heart one, but she insisted. What if she breaks up with Gabe tomorrow? She'd be stuck with his name on her arm until—"

He crossed his arms. "What were you thinking?" *She didn't have a clue what she'd done was wrong.* Frustration surged through him.

Worry settled on her face as she stepped back. "I thought it looked very professional. She'll probably start a new trend at school."

"You knew I didn't want my daughter to get a tattoo, yet *you* did it anyway. What you did will only spur on her desire for more tattoos. This," he pointed from her to him, "whatever we had between us is over. And stay away from my daughter." If he couldn't trust her where his daughter was concerned they had no future.

Her mouth dropped open, but he wasn't sticking around to argue. He slipped on the helmet, straddled the bike and fired up the engine. *I'm sorry, Lord. I tried to be civil*. He never wanted to see Hope again. It would be too painful to see her and know there could never be anything between them.

Hope's stomach sickened. *What just happened?* She stared in the direction Derrick had ridden.

Overwhelming hurt, much like she'd felt when she found out about her mother's betrayal, seared her.

Why was Derrick so upset? He acted like she'd scarred his daughter for life. *Oh no!* She pulled out her cell and called Alyssa.

"Hello."

"It's Hope. Did you tell your dad the tattoos are henna and only temporary?"

"I didn't have a chance. He rushed out of here so fast. He's been gone a long time. I'm worried." Her voice caught. "What if something happened to him?"

"Sweetie, I know your mom died in a car crash, but you can't live in fear that the same thing will happen to your dad."

"But he's been gone too long."

"He left here a minute ago. I'm sure he'll be riding

up to your house soon."

"Oh. Okay. Thanks." She sniffled. "I'm sorry for crying like a baby, but I don't want to lose my dad in a wreck too. Aunt Jill is great, but she's not my mom, you know?"

Maybe if she kept Alyssa on the phone long enough, the teen would feel more composed by the time her dad got home. "I can't say I know how you're feeling right now because I haven't lost a parent, at least not to death, but I did lose my grandma. We were very close. She died seven years ago, and I still miss her."

"My mom's been gone four, but I miss her every day. Especially when my dad goes all dictator on me. He didn't say anything, but I could tell he was angry when he left. I wanted to go after him, but I thought it'd be best to let him cool off a little. Was he awful to you?"

Hope chuckled, relieved to hear Alyssa sounding more like herself. "Not as bad as *my* dad would have been if he thought someone had given me a permanent tattoo. Girl, you need to tell him it's only henna when he gets there."

"Or not."

Hope groaned but quickly recovered. She never imagined Alyssa wouldn't want to set the record straight. "Why would you want to keep the truth from him?" It hurt that Derrick assumed the worst. Did she really want to be with a man who didn't trust her? Maybe staying away from both Derrick and his daughter would be best.

"He didn't give me a chance to explain. He should've

known they weren't real. He's being a hothead. If he's going to be so ridiculous then let him figure it out for himself that they're fake." She giggled. "I can't wait to see the look on his face when he discovers the truth. My way is much more fun."

"For whom?" She didn't like Alyssa's plan—at all. "It's kind of mean, no matter how inappropriate his response, to let him believe something that's not true. If we all received the kind of treatment we deserved, we would be very unhappy. Let's show him some grace. He's pretty mad at me, and I feel badly about that."

"Don't worry, Hope. He never stays angry long. He's going to think this is super funny once he realizes the tattoos are only temporary."

Or not. Unease gripped her. After the kiss they'd shared earlier she'd been convinced he was the one. But now, she wasn't so sure. She had tossed around Zoe's idea to stay on the island all afternoon, but after the tattoo fiasco she wasn't so sure she'd be welcome. If Derrick could push her aside so easily, maybe he wasn't the one after all.

"You still there, Hope?"

"I'm here. Just thinking."

"Good. Stop worrying and trust me. I know my dad, and he will find this funny in the end. It'll all be okay."

Maybe she was right. Jill had said the same thing, and she'd been right. Derrick didn't hold onto anger. Hopefully this time wouldn't be an exception. "Okay, but for the record, I don't like this, Alyssa. If it was me, I'd want to know the truth."

"You won't tell him, will you?" Concern edged her voice.

She wanted to connect with this girl. Then again what was the point since Derrick had told her to stay away. Was all of this really worth the emotional toll? She sighed. "If it comes up, I won't lie to your dad, but based on what he said when he left here today, I won't be seeing him anytime soon." The fact that Derrick had dropped her like a hot wire, over something like this, hurt. She really needed to rethink things regarding him.

"Thank you! You're the best!" She squealed into the phone. "Dad's here. Gotta go. Bye."

Her heart warmed toward the teen, but she still felt uneasy about the entire situation. Especially since Derrick was seriously angry with her. How could he be so dense? He had to know those tattoos weren't the real deal. Was there more going on here than she realized?

CHAPTER TEN

DERRICK STALKED INTO HIS HOUSE FILLED with regret after his encounter with Hope. But still he'd been watching out for and protecting his daughter her entire life, and Hope needed to understand that some things had to be run by him first. Period. In spite of that, he never should have talked to her like that. He could have handled his anger and frustration so much better and explained why he was upset.

"Dad!" Alyssa rushed into the entryway. "You were gone forever."

He glanced at his watch. "It was less than an hour." He noted her red-rimmed eyes, and his heart rate picked up. "Is everything okay here?"

"Yes. I was worried. I'm glad you're home."

He patted her shoulder as he passed by her on his way to the kitchen. "Do you care to discuss your tattoos?"

"Not really." She followed after him.

He pulled out a kitchen table chair. "Take a seat."

Alyssa frowned and plopped down. She crossed her

arms and wouldn't make eye contact.

Maybe right now wasn't the best time to confront her on the dangers of allowing someone to put ink on her skin. He only wanted her to be safe and healthy, but clearly she was upset, so it would keep. "Have you had dinner?"

She shook her head. "I'm not hungry. I sampled what I made at the B&B."

"Fine. I'll be in my office." He strode to the small room and closed the door. Now what was he going to do? It wouldn't be right for Alyssa to think she got away with this, but at the same time, he wanted her to be honest with him—tell him that the tattoos weren't real and understand she should run things like this by him first.

She had to know at first glance he believed they were the real deal. Why didn't she say anything?

He sat at his desk. He needed to deal with Hope too, but he'd made such a mess of things with her. He winced at the memory of his harsh words. Maybe it would be best to steer clear of her for a day or two and give them both time to regroup and then in a few days clear the air—if that was possible. He'd allowed years of built up fear that he was inadequate as a single parent to come to a head and combust today. It might be too late to repair the damage, even if he gave Hope a little space.

Hope worried her bottom lip while sitting on the porch swing at the bed and breakfast. Derrick hadn't spoken one word to her since Saturday, four whole days ago, when she'd painted the tattoo on Alyssa. She and her crew took a job off the island yesterday since they were waiting for some of the cabins to be dry-walled.

The front door of the B&B door opened, and Jill stepped outside with a broom. "Oh, hi. I didn't realize you were out here. I can sweep later." She turned to go.

"Don't mind me."

Jill glanced her way then did a double take. Her face softened. "Why so glum?"

Hope shrugged.

"Mind if I join you?"

She shifted to one side of the swing.

"I've heard what you've been dealing with. I'm sorry about your house. Has any progress been made on rebuilding it?"

She shook her head. "Not really. I have an old friend drawing up the design for the new house, but these things take time. I don't know what I'm going to do. Once this job is up, I'll have no place to live until my house is finished. I considered rebuilding and selling my home in Tacoma so I could get a place here instead, but now I'm not sure what I want to do. I've come to love this island and the community here in spite of the problems I've encountered."

"You don't have to buy a place to live on the island. We have rentals." Jill's face lit. "I happen to know of one that would be perfect for you while you wait for your house to be rebuilt. Rachel and her husband Chris have a rental unit at their house."

"I don't know, Jill. It's a big decision to stay here. I have a lot to consider. I thought it was what I wanted, but things have changed." She desired to stay more than anything, but what if Alyssa was wrong and Derrick never forgave her for the tattoos?

On top of that, she obviously cared more about him than he did for her if he could so easily cut her from his life. If she stayed, would it hurt too much to see Derrick?

"If by things changing, you're talking about my brother and Alyssa, stop worrying. He's a stubborn man, but he'll eventually realize he was wrong to get so angry, and he'll come to his senses."

"Alyssa told you about the henna."

"She didn't have to. I could tell by looking at them. I'm pretty sure Derrick knows the tattoos aren't real, but he's too prideful to admit he messed up and overreacted—at least he hasn't said anything to me." She shook her head. "This is so unlike him to behave this way. He's normally very levelheaded. I guess when it comes to his daughter the papa bear comes out in him." She lowered her voice. "Don't you tell a soul, but I once gave myself a henna tattoo. I was twelve and had a crush on a boy at school. I put our initials in a heart on my thigh where no one would see it."

"You're kidding!"

"I'm not. To this day, it's the craziest thing I've ever done. I know she doesn't want her dad to know they're temporary, so I'm avoiding the topic whenever I see him."

"He blames me," Hope said softly. "He actually thinks I would give his daughter a permanent tattoo. As if I would or even could do something like that." If she didn't feel so badly about it all, she'd be angry with him for his assumption—it was insulting. But all she felt was sad.

"I won't make excuses for my brother, but I hope you will decide to stay on in Wildflower."

"Your brother has made it very clear I am not welcome here." Well, at least she was not welcome in his life.

"My brother is one person among several hundred. Are you really going to allow a stubborn man to dictate where you live?" She sighed. "I thought you were stronger than that."

"Apparently I'm not."

"Why do you care what Derrick thinks anyway? My niece adores you. She raced into my room to show me the tattoos you gave her right after you did them. You're quite the artist. In fact, your style reminds me of a metal artist whose work I love. H.L."

"You're a fan of H.L.?"

"You know his work?" Excitement lit Jill's voice. "His designs are timeless. There are a couple of his pieces at the resort. The motion he creates is amazing. I only wish I had discovered his work before he dropped off the planet."

"You keep referring to H.L. as a he, but the artist is a

she."

Jill's eyes widened. "You're kidding. I have no idea why I assumed she was a he. I feel silly for not knowing, considering I'm such a fan. But I detest research, so I guess that explains my mistake. Anyway, I don't know what it is exactly about Alyssa's tattoos that reminds me of H.L."

Clearly, Jill was trying to make her feel better, but it wasn't working. By choosing to honor Alyssa's request she'd ruined whatever hope she and Derrick had. Work today was tense to say the least when their paths crossed. Goose flesh broke out on her arms. She ran her hands up and down them.

"These spring evenings can be cool. The house is nice and comfy if you want to go inside and warm up."

"Thanks, Jill, but I think I'll go for a drive instead." She'd heard the coffee at The General Store was excellent, and the change of scenery would be nice.

Derrick pushed the lawnmower back and forth across his backyard. He'd left Alyssa and Gabe inside working on homework. He ought to ground her from seeing him, but since they were studying, it didn't seem like an appropriate punishment. He could easily check on them through the large window in the kitchen, to make sure they stayed on task.

Alyssa stood and pulled open the door. She ran her finger across her throat.

He cut the engine. "What's up?"

"Can we go get ice cream at The General Store?"

He frowned. "No. There's ice cream in the freezer. Help yourselves."

"But, Dad—"

He pulled the chord on the mower, and it roared back to life. Alyssa had to learn that actions had consequences. His thoughts drifted to Hope. Regret still churned in his gut. Even though emotions had been high, he probably should have talked to her days ago, so she understood why he was upset. He'd even had an opportunity at work two days ago, but couldn't find the words. He'd determined yesterday to get it over with, but couldn't find her. Now bringing it up felt even harder.

He killed the engine then pushed the mower inside the shed. A rustling from the corner of the shed alerted his senses. His adrenaline spiked. What if it was a skunk? A skunk had sprayed him once, and it was not an experience he cared to repeat.

"Dad?"

"Stay back! There's something in here." He grabbed a shovel and prayed whatever was there wasn't a skunk or an opossum.

Gabe stepped up beside her. "I saw a cat in the yard earlier."

Derrick shook his head. "We don't have a cat." Soft mewing sounded from the corner. "Then again maybe we do." He pushed aside a few boxes and sure enough a momma cat and her kittens lay snuggled into the corner. "Come see."

Alyssa squatted in front of the little family. "They're so cute. Can we keep them?" She looked at him with eyes that were virtually impossible to say no to.

"Those kittens will grow up into cats. We can't have three cats."

"Don't forget the momma. That'd make four," Gabe said. "We could probably take one."

"Hold on a minute. That cat probably belongs to someone." Derrick peered closer in the dimly lit shed but couldn't spot a collar.

"We could take pictures, make a flier and hang it in town." Alyssa reached her hand out and ran it down the cat's back then reached for one of the kittens. "He's so soft."

The last thing they needed was a kitten, but he had to admit the little thing was pretty cute. The solid white Momma cat was pretty too. The island didn't have an animal shelter so that wasn't an option. "I wonder how momma is getting food. She looks healthy."

"Could be a mouser," Gabe said. "Or maybe the cat lives nearby and came here to have her kittens."

"Maybe. I like your sign idea, Alyssa. Why don't you and Gabe get right on that?"

She beamed a smile up at him, put the kitten back, then pulled out her cell phone from her jeans pocket. "Look at the camera, kitty." A light flashed, and the cat hissed. Alyssa yelped and hopped back. "Sorry ol' girl. Didn't mean to startle you." She stood and showed him and Gabe the picture. "Looks good. Right?"

Gabe nodded. "Her pure white coloring is nice. Someone is bound to know where she belongs."

"Unless she was left here by a tourist." Not that pet abandonment had been much of an issue, but Derrick had heard about a dog that had been left behind a while back.

Alyssa pushed up her sleeves revealing her tattoos. Derrick winced. Would those things ever wash off? At least he didn't have to worry about an allergic reaction any longer. She would have had a rash by now if she had an allergy to the ink. Jenna had had very sensitive skin, and even after her death he continued to buy the same scent free products she'd purchased.

Later that afternoon, Derrick handed Jill a glass of water then eased down onto the couch in his family room. His sister had dropped by unexpectedly, and from the storm brewing on her face he knew he was in trouble. But what had he done?

Jill sipped the water then placed it on the end table beside the chair she occupied. "I heard you found kittens?"

He nodded.

"What are you going to do with them?"

"Alyssa and Gabe are trying to find the cat's owner. They went to town to hang up signs."

"Good." She folded her hands in her lap.

"Out with it. You're wearing your stern schoolteacher face. What's going on?"

She chuckled. "You, dear brother, are an idiot."

"Excuse me?" He leaned forward. "What did I do to

deserve that?"

"I'm talking about Hope."

His jaw tensed. "Oh. She's not open for discussion."

"Good, because I only need you to listen. She's going through a rough time right now. Did it ever occur to you that by doing something nice for someone else it makes her feel better?"

He shook his head. "I'm sorry, but I'm lost. I think you'd better start over."

"Hope is a caring woman who only wanted to make your daughter happy."

"I know, but—"

"No buts! Now you listen and listen well. Those tattoos are henna."

"I know."

"It's a temporary ink that lasts a week or two." She suddenly stopped talking and stared at him. "Wait. You know? Why didn't you say anything?"

"I was angry that she'd tattoo my daughter without at least asking my permission. What if Alyssa had been allergic and had a reaction? Her actions could have hurt my daughter." His stomach knotted and his face heated. "I wanted to give it a few days and let emotions settle down. I tried to find Hope yesterday to clear the air, but she wasn't around. I've been otherwise occupied today."

"Of all the stupid ideas you've had, this has got to be on top." She shook her head. "For a smart man you can be dense at times. Hope would *never* do anything to harm you or your daughter. Where is this coming from?"

"I know that Hope wouldn't deliberately hurt Alyssa,

and it doesn't matter why I temporarily showed poor judgment." His sister didn't need to know the root of his insecurity. He thought back to the women he'd overheard talking about his inadequate skills as a dad shortly after his wife had died. It still hurt that he'd been the topic of the gossips, but they'd been right. He wasn't a good mom, but he'd worked hard to fill the gap and felt like he'd done an adequate job too, at least until recently. Now everything was messed up.

He ran his hand down his face and stood, pacing to the window then back to the couch. He never should have waited to clear the air between them. Hope must hate him. He swallowed the lump in his throat.

"What are you going to do?"

"I need to find Hope and talk to her. This is not the kind of conversation I want to have over the phone."

She smiled. "Good. Then my work here is done. Oh, and don't forget about Easter dinner at the B&B on Sunday."

"I won't. And thanks." Somehow he needed to get Hope to forgive him.

CHAPTER ELEVEN

Hope pulled up to The General Store and hopped out of her SUV. She'd spent scant time in the heart of Wildflower, which needed to change if she was going to seriously consider living here.

Alyssa and Gabe stepped outside, each holding a small stack of paper.

"Hi, you two. What're you doing?"

"We found a stray cat with kittens in our shed so we made fliers to hang up around town." She handed Hope the flier.

"Oh, they look so sweet."

Alyssa sighed. "They are. If we don't find the mama cat's owner, we'll need to find good homes for the kittens. Would you like one if it comes to that?"

Hope shook her head. "I don't have a home right now. I can't have a kitten, no matter how adorable."

Alyssa's face fell. "I forgot about your house burning down." She raised the stack of fliers. "We should get these put up."

"Sure. See you." Hope moved aside then went into

the shop. She stopped in the entryway too surprised to enter further. She'd heard this place was like stepping back in time, but she hadn't truly believed it until this moment.

Wood flooring that had seen better days creaked as she stepped forward and off to the right where the café was situated. She walked up to the register and studied the board listing the kind of coffee drinks available.

A teenage girl walked up to the counter. "What can I get for you?"

"I'm a latte person. What do you recommend?"

"Our vanilla latte is good. Or maybe you'd like our chai tea latte. It's pretty popular." She described it.

Hope glanced at the menu board once more. "I'm normally not a tea person, but that sounds delicious. I'll take a small one please." She paid then stepped aside to check out the rest of the area as her drink was prepared.

The other side of the store was a grocery of sorts, but probably only had the basics considering it was no larger than a mini-mart. And this side, though rustic, wasn't as old fashioned as she'd first thought. She noted the jukebox against the wall and grinned—then again, it was like stepping back in time.

"Here's your chai tea latte." The teen slid her drink across the counter.

"Thanks. Does the jukebox work?"

"Yep. We've only had it a few months. It's pretty popular with the weekend crowds."

Hope stifled a laugh. She hadn't seen any crowds

since she'd been on the island, but Wildflower had a reputation for being a summer destination. "Maybe I'll stop in on a weekend sometime." She raised her drink. "Thanks."

Her cell phone rang, and she pulled it from her pocket. "Hi, Duncan. How are things?"

"Not bad. I have the plans for your house ready for your approval. When can we meet?"

"How about tomorrow morning? I can sneak away, but we'd have to meet someplace near the ferry."

"You're still doing that job on Wildflower Island?"

"Yep."

"Okay. Let's meet at Cuppa Beans at ten." He had farther to travel than she did, so even though that messed up her morning, she'd roll with it.

"Sounds good. See you tomorrow." She moved her thumb to disconnect the call but was momentarily distracted.

"Are you doing okay, Hope?" His voice filled with concern.

"I've been better, but you're making this a lot easier. I'll see you."

"Okay. Bye."

Duncan knew her too well. They'd been friends for a long time.

She'd wanted to explore this island since arriving. Today was the day, and no one would interrupt. She powered off her phone and headed to her SUV. Going off grid for the rest of the day would keep anyone and everyone from disturbing her, which was exactly what she needed. A day to herself to think and soak in the island.

The following day Hope drove off the ferry onto the mainland. Her heart wasn't into dealing with the plans for her house, but regardless, decisions had to be made.

A short time later, she pulled into the Cuppa Beans lot, parked and wandered inside. The rich scent of coffee greeted her. A low hum of voices filled the air. Looking around the open space, she spotted Duncan at a corner table with his laptop and a cylinder that probably contained the paper plans.

She waved and wove her way through scattered wood tables and chairs and stopped beside the one where her longtime friend waited. "'Good morning, Duncan. Thanks for agreeing to meet me here. I know it was a bit of a drive for you."

Well-dressed in a tailored suit, Duncan stood and hugged her. "No problem. Did you want to order a drink?"

"Good idea. Can I get you something?"

He pointed to a mug on the table.

"I missed that. Be right back." She pivoted and moved to the register. "I'd like a chai tea latte, please." Hopefully this place would make it as delicious as the one she'd had yesterday. She paid and waited for it. A few minutes later she returned to the table, pulled up a chair beside Duncan, and sat so she could see the computer.

He woke up the screen and immediately went through his design plan.

"I like it." She knew he was the one for the job. He got her and that made working with him a breeze.

"Great. Once the city approves the plan, things can get rolling."

"Sounds good. How've you been?"

"Not bad. Keeping busy. I appreciate you asking me to design your home."

"Of course. You know I'm a fan of your work."

"I'm a fan of yours as well. Anything new on the horizon?"

She shook her head and tried to ignore the look of dismay on his face as she took a long drink of her tea.

"I heard a rumor you might move to Wildflower Island."

She nearly spewed out her drink but stopped herself in time. "Who told you that?"

"I saw Chase Grayson the other day."

Duncan had gone to school with her and Piper, so it made sense he'd know Piper's husband. They'd all stayed close through the years. "Piper wants me to, but I'm not yet sure it's a good idea."

"Why's that?"

She shrugged and took another long drink from her cup.

He raised a brow, clearly not willing to let her off the hook.

"It's complicated."

"Complicated?" He frowned, and then his face cleared. "You're involved with someone!" His blue eyes twinkled. "It's about time you trusted someone enough to fall for him."

"Oh, stop. I don't have a boyfriend. And I don't have trust issues."

He raised a brow. "Yeah right. You might be able to fool yourself, but I know differently." He finished off his coffee then stood. "When you figure out if you are staying or selling let me know. We don't want the finishes to be too taste specific if you're going to put it on the market."

She stood and gathered her belongings. "Good point. You have my contractor's contact information, and you'll stay on top of everything for me?"

"Of course. That's what friends are for."

"Thank you. It's a relief knowing someone I trust has everything handled for me."

He stood and dropped a peck on her cheek. "I know you said you aren't involved with anyone, but I have a feeling you're in denial about your feelings for someone. Follow your heart. I'd hate to see you miss out on your Mr. Right."

"You're being silly." Hope resisted squirming in her seat.

"Trust me, I know what I'm talking about. You're the one that got away, and I kick myself at least once a month."

She chuckled as her face heated. Duncan liked to

exaggerate. They'd had exactly three dates in college, then decided they'd make better friends than a couple. They walked side by side to the parking lot.

He pressed a button on his key fob and pulled open his door. "I'll be in touch."

She nodded and strode to her SUV. If she hurried, she'd make the ferry and not have to wait for the next one. Her thoughts drifted to Duncan's exclamation that she was involved with a man. If he'd said that before the henna incident she might have agreed. But now . . . she couldn't entertain the idea. Not if Derrick could so easily shut her out of his life. Besides, she'd always said she'd never get involved with a man with children. Alyssa wasn't exactly a child, but it was clear having another person involved complicated things. She should have stuck with her resolve to never get involved with a dad and spared herself the heartache of rejection.

The ferry line ahead only had two cars. She pulled up behind a sports car. The ferry docked and a few cars drove off. She followed the car in front of her, then parked and walked to the railing. A light breeze lifted the hair off her neck and cooled her cheeks. Seagulls soared overhead fishing for food.

Duncan would do his best to make sure everything moved along smoothly with her house until she finished her job on the island, but then what? Although she managed to get along with her mother, there was no way she could live under the same roof with her while her house was being built.

She had a few friends who might let her crash at

their place, but she didn't like being a burden. Renting was an option, but what a pain to set up house only to move again once her home was finished.

Lord, what do I do?

Derrick finished helping a guest then turned to his right-hand man. "I'm going to grab lunch and take a drive out to the cabins to check on things. Call if you need me."

"Sounds good, boss. I can handle this."

"I'm counting on it." Noon was generally a slow time of day. He'd tried several times over the past two days to locate Hope. Had even stopped by the cabins yesterday to see her, and discovered she'd gone to an appointment off the island. Then in the evening he'd had to work late, and when he'd gotten home Alyssa needed homework help. He'd not had another opportunity to talk with Hope. He could call, but he wanted to have their conversation face-to-face.

He hopped into his pickup and headed the short distance up to the cabins. The cul-de-sac where the cabins were situated was quiet today. It must be because of the holiday weekend. He frowned. Where was Hope's SUV?

Disappointment washed over him. He owed her an apology, but maybe it was better if he didn't try to pick up where they'd left off. He had Alyssa to consider, even though she'd given her blessing. And work was demanding on his time. In addition, Hope would be leaving soon. He didn't have the energy or time to work at a long distance relationship.

With a sigh, he parked in front of the cabin her crew had been working on yesterday. As long as he was here he might as well check out their progress. He unlocked the door, stepped into the eight-hundred square foot unit and quickly looked over the electrical work.

A shadow in the doorway blocked the sunshine from filtering in. He turned. "Hope." His heart raced. "I was looking for you."

"Here I am." She stood tall. "What can I do for you?"

"Forgive me?"

"Come again?"

"We need to talk. Do you have a few minutes?"

"Okay."

"I overreacted about the tattoos. I'm sorry."

She crossed her arms. "You finally realized they weren't permanent, huh?"

He nodded. "Actually I only believed they were real to begin with. About halfway here it occurred to me, there was no way you could have given her a real tattoo. It didn't take long to realize they weren't. Fear spurred my anger when I confronted you, and I regret that. I've been looking out for my daughter her whole life, and what you did scared me. Her mother had extremely sensitive skin, and I didn't know if Alyssa would have a reaction. I've heard horror stories about some ink and I was scared."

"Oh. I didn't think of that. I'm sorry. I should have

checked with you first, but an allergy never crossed my mind."

"I know. Please forgive me for overreacting."

"Okay."

That's it? "All right, then. I guess I'll see you Sunday at the B&B's Easter meal."

She nodded and stepped aside so he could leave.

Why had he thought apologizing would make everything okay between them? Clearly he'd hurt her more than he'd realized. How was he supposed to fix it?

CHAPTER TWELVE

Hope sat beside her bedroom window with her Bible in hand staring out over Puget Sound. To her way of thinking, Easter was a day to contemplate what Jesus had done. That he would suffer so much for her and everyone else still boggled her mind. That was true love—love like no other.

Per her Easter tradition, she opened her Bible to the book of Luke and began reading in chapter 22, verse 39 through the first part of chapter 24. Anguish for Jesus gripped her, and her throat thickened from unshed tears. No matter how many times she read this passage it affected her the same way.

Jesus' love was almost unfathomable. How He could suffer so that imperfect people like herself, her mother, and Derrick could go to heaven amazed her. The words to the song *Jesus Messiah* by Chris Tomlin filled her mind for a few moments. The Lord's amazing love overwhelmed her. The tears streamed freely. That song perfectly summed up what Jesus had done.

She dried her eyes then finished reading the

passage. After a few moments of quiet, she allowed her mind to drift to the events of the day ahead. First she'd attend church and then the Easter meal here at the bed-and-breakfast. Her stomach fluttered. Derrick would be there. She'd done her best to avoid him, but she'd have no choice today.

A knock at her door drew her attention. "Who is it?"

"Jill. May I let myself in?"

"Sure." What could Derrick's sister want? She faced the door, and her eyes widened as Jill came into view holding a tray complete with delicious smelling food and a small vase holding tulips. "What's this?"

"The flowers are from my brother, but the meal in your room was my idea. It's a madhouse downstairs, and I figured you'd prefer to eat in here."

Derrick sent flowers? Now that she thought about it, the B&B did seem noisier than usual. A family of five checked in yesterday and sadly the children were less than well behaved. "That was thoughtful of you." She noted a coffee carafe, two mugs, and a platter piled high with scrambled eggs, bacon and some kind of a potato dish. Another plate held two cinnamon rolls. "There is no way I will be able to eat all of this."

Jill chuckled. "I was counting on that. Do you mind if I join you?" She pulled a second plate from under the first.

"Not at all. I take it you need a break from the racket downstairs?"

Jill nodded and served herself. "It's my day off. Most of the time eating breakfast in the dining room isn't a big deal. I often eat in the kitchen, too, but today . . . let's just say I needed some peace. I figured you wouldn't mind."

Hope grinned. "Not at all. Who can complain about room service?"

"Don't forget the flowers." Jill forked a bite of scrambled eggs into her mouth.

She was trying *not* to think about the flowers.

"Derrick never gives anyone flowers. No one has ever made him work hard enough that he felt the need."

"What about his wife?" Hope dug into the eggs too.

Jill shook her head. "Maybe on Valentine's Day. It was love at first sight for them." Jill poured coffee into their mugs, then added cream and sugar to her own.

"Oh." She'd never believed in love at first sight, but respected Derrick enough to give him the benefit of the doubt. Too bad she couldn't have been so blessed in the love department.

Jill stirred her coffee then set the spoon on a saucer. "May I ask you a personal question?"

She stilled. "I suppose so. But I may choose not to answer." She sipped the coffee hoping to hide how nervous Jill's request made her.

"Fair enough. I'm not normally such a busy body, but I love my brother, imperfections and all, and I'm concerned that the two of you are missing out on something wonderful because of the henna incident." Her face shone a pretty pink that complemented her dark hair, which hung in soft waves down her back.

Hope took another sip then slowly set the mug on

the table. "You certainly speak your mind." She had no desire to get into this with Derrick's sister, but maybe it would help. Ever since he apologized, she'd been struggling with letting go of the hurt she was holding onto. "I always told myself that I'd never get involved with a dad. That kids complicate relationships."

"It would seem that way in this case." Jill gave her a sad smile.

"You're right, but when it came to Derrick, I broke my rule and fell for him."

Her face lit. "That's great!"

Hope shook her head. "When Derrick chose to believe the worst about me, it brought up past pain that I'm still dealing with." She realized he'd reacted out of fear for his daughter, but if he hadn't been so angry to begin with thinking she'd actually given Alyssa a real tattoo, she believed a calmer head would have prevailed.

"I'm so sorry, Hope. I had no idea."

She shrugged. "It's not that I don't care for him, because I do. But I already have one person in my life that I love who has hurt me so deeply it changed me to my core. I don't want to get involved with a man who can't trust me and believe the best in me as his *first* instinct." Maybe she desired the impossible, but one thing was certain—she would not settle. She wanted unconditional love.

"Who hurt you?" Jill studied her face as if the answer was plastered across her forehead.

Hope looked down. "It doesn't matter." Talking about

her mom and what she did never helped and only served to make her feel worse because her own mother thought so little of her.

"I feel like it matters a lot. If I'd hurt you, I don't think it would be so life altering, so I'm guessing it was someone close to you. Someone you trusted implicitly."

Hope's throat thickened once again. Her appetite now gone, she placed the fork on her plate and folded her hands in her lap.

"The only kind of person that has that kind of control is someone you love deeply. Like a parent, family member or a man you love."

She sighed. "It was my mom. Now can we please drop it?"

"Consider it dropped." Jill raised the mug to her lips and took a long sip before setting it back on the table. "Have you seen the kittens Derrick found in his shed? They are so adorable. Pure white."

Whoa. When Jill changed a subject she took a leap. "I only saw the black and white flier Alyssa and Gabe made."

"Oh. That didn't do them justice. They are so precious and their momma takes the best care of them. We're guessing they're about three or four weeks old, but it's hard to know for sure. I had a cat growing up, and when she had her one and only litter it amazed me how dependent the kittens were on her for their very survival. Princess was the best cat."

"That's a pretty name."

Jill nodded. "Thanks. She was beautiful too. Snow

white like the ones in the shed." She chuckled. "Although Princess was a great mom, she wasn't perfect. I'll never forget the day she almost killed one of her kittens."

Hope's breath caught. "Seriously? What happened?"

"I was young and didn't understand that I shouldn't hold the kittens. In an effort to protect her kittens she picked them up by the neck to move them to what she probably thought was a safer location. The only problem was I freaked out when I saw it in her mouth and tried to take it from her, but she held tighter. When she finally let go it lay limp and unmoving. I was devastated."

Hope's heart broke at the vivid pain in Jill's eyes. "But you said *almost* killed."

"Right. I was young, so it's all a little fuzzy, but the kitten ended up being okay. My mom said that it was my fault Princess panicked. I felt horrible. I eventually had to forgive myself because the guilt literally made me sick. Kind of like Derrick is doing to himself."

Hope drew in a sharp breath. "What is Derrick feeling guilty about?"

"Overreacting. He feels horrible. He's actually lost a few pounds."

"He told you that?" Now *she* felt bad.

Jill finished off the rest of her coffee. "That was the best meal. I would work here forever, as long as Zoe is the one cooking." She stood and gathered the dishes. "I need to get ready for church. Will you be there?" She removed the flowers from the tray and placed them on the table.

Hope nodded, strode to the door, and pulled it open. "Thanks for breakfast and for the talk."

"It's always nice to change things up." Jill left without a backward glance.

As Hope hurried to get ready for the Easter service, her mind was on Derrick the whole time. She had no idea he was making himself sick over her. Even though she didn't see a future for them as a couple, the air needed to be cleared, and it was up to her to do it.

Thirty minutes later she slid into the pew at church a few rows behind Derrick. It wouldn't be long, and there'd be no place left to sit. The worship leader invited everyone to stand, opened with a modern rendition of *Amazing Grace* then moved on to *He Lives* and ended with *Christ the Lord is Risen Today*.

Pastor Michaels stepped onto the stage. "He is risen!"

"He is risen indeed," they all replied.

"Please be seated."

Hope settled in for the sermon.

"Because He lives we have hope." He went on to talk about forgiveness.

Hope's mind wandered—forgiveness. She'd forgiven her mom and Derrick. That wasn't her problem. Letting go of the hurt was. How was she supposed to forget? Maybe forgetting wasn't necessary, but something had to give for her to be able to move past the hurt.

The sermon wrapped up. A short time later she made her way to the rear of the sanctuary. She found a spot along the wall, near the door where Derrick should exit. Person after person left, but there was no sign of Derrick. What happened to him? She poked her head inside and sighed. Somehow she'd missed him.

She turned and walked leisurely toward the parking lot. She'd really hoped to talk with him. The idea that he was torturing himself because of her was too much. He needed to know that she forgave him.

"Hope!"

She looked over her shoulder and spotted Alyssa waving. Hope stopped and waited for the teen to catch up. "Happy Easter."

"Same to you. Did you hear the news?" Her face lit with excitement.

Hope shook her head.

"We found the cat's owner."

"That's great. I'm sure they were relieved to have her back."

"I think so. Although they were surprised about the kittens. The cat's name is May. Her birthday is in May, so they named her May."

"Original."

Alyssa giggled. "You're going to be at the Easter meal at the B&B right?"

"I wouldn't miss it."

"Good. See you." She turned and darted away before Hope could ask her about her dad.

She pulled out her cell phone and typed in a message to Derrick. *Can we talk? I'll be on the beach below the B&B in twenty minutes.* She pressed Send, hoping he would look at his phone. If he was anything like her, he silenced or turned it off during services, and rarely remembered to change the setting right after church. Many a Sunday she'd missed calls and texts.

She slid into her SUV and headed to the B&B. A few minutes later she parked and went straight to the beach. There was no reason to change out of her sundress and sweater since the meal would be served in a little more than an hour.

Seagulls soared overhead as she made her way along the path that led to the beach. Although nervous energy demanded she keep moving, a large boulder perfect for sitting seemed the better option. If Derrick showed, she wouldn't miss him. He still hadn't replied to her text.

She perched on the boulder and stared at the water. A fish leaped. She gasped. Then an Orca breached the surface followed by a second one not far off shore. She stood and raced to the shoreline while holding up her cellphone to capture the whales. Her heart raced as she pressed record. The whale breached the water again only higher this time. *This is so cool!*

"Pretty amazing, huh?"

Hope jumped and whirled to her left. "Derrick! I didn't realize you were there." She stopped recording.

"I got your text. I've wanted to talk with you since we spoke at the cabins the other day."

"You have?"

"Yes. But first, you wanted to talk about something?"

She turned from watching the whales. "I did." She

trudged back to the boulder and sat. "I wanted to thank you for the flowers. They were beautiful and very thoughtful."

"It was the least I could do." He reached out and grasped her hand, cradling it between his. "I'm so sorry. I really messed up. I should never have confronted you the way I did. Will you please forgive me?"

"I forgive you. And you don't have to keep apologizing."

"Then why do things feel so awkward between us?" His brow furrowed.

"Your first instinct was to believe the worst."

He looked confused.

She took a breath and let it out in a quick puff. "The thing is this. When my mom did what she did, even though I've forgiven her, it changed me. I hate getting hurt, so I have a difficult time trusting a person once I've been burned." She shook her head. "That's not completely correct. I have a hard time trusting period."

"So it's not only me? And here I thought I was special." He grinned, clearly trying to lighten the mood.

"You're special all right." She smirked at him teasingly. "But in all seriousness, I want you to know I truly forgive you, but I struggle moving past hurts. When you chose to believe the worst about me it changed things between us, but I have forgiven you so there is no reason for you to hold onto the guilt. This is my problem, not yours."

"Is there any chance we can go back to the way things were?" He rubbed the back of his neck. "I know that probably sounds impossible. In fact, a few days ago, I didn't want to pick up where we left off, but I've come to realize I need you in my life."

Her stomach clenched. She wanted that more than anything. But was that realistic? Yes, she was fond of him. But was that enough? "I don't know, Derrick. Will you always jump to conclusions and believe the worst about me before even trying to find out the truth?"

"I've learned my lesson. Did I mention how sorry I am?"

She chuckled. "I think that's been covered."

"How about this?" Using his forefinger, he guided her head to face him, then dropped his hand to his side. "I can't promise I will never hurt you again, but I do promise to give you the benefit of the doubt in the future and talk with you before drawing conclusions. And in return, I'd appreciate if you'd run things by me that have to do with Alyssa."

"I think I could manage that." In his position she'd want the same consideration. She nodded. "And I would like that." But a part of her still hesitated. "But what guarantee do I have that you won't slip up?"

"You don't. I'm not perfect."

She cared deeply for this man, and his honesty and openness made turning her back on him impossible. "Okay."

"Okay? You'll give me another chance, or okay I'm not perfect?"

She grinned. "Both. How about we start over?" She thrust out her hand. "I'm Hope Michaels. And you are?" She raised a brow.

CHAPTER THIRTEEN

Start over? The Puget Sound to her back, Derrick stared at Hope's outstretched hand. He wanted to pick up where they'd left off, but if she needed there to be a blank slate he was willing to accommodate. At least she didn't tell him to get out of her life. "Derrick Trainor. It's a pleasure to meet you. What brings you to Wildflower Island?"

"A job. A longtime friend of mine begged me to come work at her resort."

A chuckle escaped.

She playfully slapped his arm. "Be serious."

He laughed. "I'm trying, but this is kind of silly."

She frowned.

"I'll try harder. So you are working at the resort. I happen to be the acting manager there now. Funny we haven't met sooner."

She laughed. "Okay. I guess this *is* silly. But I want a fresh start without all the baggage."

"Sweetheart." He ran his thumb along her jawline. "The past will always be there, but what you choose to do with those memories is up to you. Starting over or picking up where we left off isn't going to change that." He took her hand and laced his fingers through hers. "Let's take a walk, then we'd better head to the bed-and-breakfast. We don't want to be late for the meal." Clearly she needed time to consider his words.

"Sounds good. I heard you found the cat's owner."

"Yes. I think Alyssa is going to miss the kittens, but I'm relieved they're gone."

"Not a cat lover?"

"No. That's not it. The kittens will need to see a vet soon, and then later we'd have to find them all homes. It was a lot of work that I don't have the time for right now."

"I hear that."

He stopped, and when she turned to face him, her questioning eyes drew him, but he instead focused on what he needed to say. "I never thanked you for making my daughter feel so special. No one has ever cared enough to take the time to get to know her greatest desire and try to make her wish come true."

Her mouth opened slightly. "Thank you, and you're welcome. Speaking of Alyssa, how is she doing?"

"Much better than she had been, thanks to you. If you hadn't given me the advice about how to deal with her boyfriend, I'm not sure my daughter and I would be on speaking terms."

Hope patted his shoulder. "She would've forgiven you eventually. Take it from me. I'm an expert when it comes to forgiving a parent."

He turned and headed back. "But yet, you still have no inspiration to create. Why is that?"

She shrugged. "Just because I forgave my mom, doesn't mean the hurt from the lies she spread about me isn't still there. The fact that my own mother would do that hurt more than if a stranger or someone else had lied about me and spread rumors. I don't know how to move past it."

She said it like it was just the way things were. As if she had no power to change. His gut twisted for her. He wanted to help her, but how? He guided them onto the path leading up to the B&B, and soon they came out onto the backyard lawn. "Did I mention how nice you look today? I've never seen you in a dress."

"Thanks. I rarely wear one, but Easter is one of those occasions that I feel like I must." She shrugged. "It's the way I was raised. Although my parents are new believers, they attended church with me from time to time when I was growing up, and on Easter Sunday we always dressed up."

"Did you go to church anytime besides?"

She nodded. "A friend invited me when I was in middle school. I loved the youth group and continued to attend until I left for college. My parents said they saw the difference attending church made in me, and out of curiosity they visited from time to time. It wasn't until this past year that they became Christians."

Derrick pushed the B&B's front door open and allowed Hope to go in first. Warm air greeted them along with the dull rumble of voices from the direction of the sitting room.

He placed a hand on her lower back and guided her toward the noise. His eyes widened at the full to capacity room. There were probably twenty-five to thirty people gathered in here. He recognized many of the guests, but there were several unfamiliar faces.

It looked like Piper had decided to break the rules this afternoon and leave her house. She sat with her back to the piano on the bench. Chase stood by her side with a hand resting on her shoulder. Rachel and Chris along with their two children were situated on the sofa. Jill worked the room with a platter of pigs in a blanket, her cheeks flushed.

His sister approached them and held out the tray. "Zoe is running behind and asked me to offer a snack to tide everyone over. You want a couple?"

He grinned. "They smell delicious." He reached for the little hot dog wrapped in what looked like a crescent roll and popped it into his mouth. *Mmm.* He loved those things.

Alyssa came into the room from the direction of the kitchen and grinned wide when her gaze rested on Hope. She rushed over. "Hope, will you help me decorate the cookies?"

Hope looked to him for a moment. "Sounds like fun, but I think your dad should help too."

"I'm game." He accompanied them to the kitchen and washed his hands. Zoe stood at the stove oblivious to them.

"I wanted to have cutout cookies for dessert even

though Zoe made a couple of pies." Alyssa waved him over to the island where she had a cookie frosting station set up, complete with sprinkles and pastry bags filled with various colored icings. Most of the cookies already had a smooth coating of shiny frosting in various colors.

"Is there any particular way we should be doing this?"

"I already put the fondant frosting on most of the cookies, but I thought it'd be fun to decorate them," Alyssa said.

Hope sidled up to him after washing her hands. "Decorate however you want, Derrick." She picked up a pastry bag and piped an intricate design onto an egg. By the time she'd finished, it reminded him of a Faberge egg. He stayed silent as she created another masterpiece.

Alyssa's eyes widened, but she also remained quiet. It looked like his daughter understood that something special was happening.

He didn't even bother to decorate a cookie. Anything he did would look like the work of a preschooler compared to what Hope was doing.

Zoe motioned to them that the food was ready, but even she seemed to understand that something special was taking place.

Without disturbing Hope they all moved from the kitchen and gathered in the dining room around the table.

Zoe's husband, Nick, offered a blessing for the food,

and they lined up to serve themselves buffet style from the sideboard.

"I know there are a lot of us, so feel free to sit here in the dining room or out on the front porch if you'd rather enjoy the sunshine."

Eating outdoors sounded nice, but he'd let his daughter decide. He glanced toward the kitchen door. When would Hope join them? Maybe he should make her a plate. No, there was more than enough food. Besides he didn't know what she liked, much less wanted. He waited his turn then piled his plate with ham, scalloped potatoes, a dinner roll, and green beans. There were several other choices, but he preferred simple food.

"Should we eat at the table or on the porch?" he asked Alyssa.

"Outside for sure." She waved her empty hand in front of her face. "It's too hot in here."

He glanced toward the kitchen. Should he get Hope?

"She's fine, Dad."

How did you—?"

"You are so easy to read. It's obvious you have the hots for her."

"Hey, keep your voice down." He pulled open the front door and led the way outside to a large table with six chairs set around it.

"You trying to deny it?"

"I didn't say that, but no one else needs to know." At least for now. Especially since he still wasn't sure where he stood with Hope.

Hope looked up from the cookie she was decorating and frowned. *Where'd everyone go?* Voices filtered in from the dining room. She placed the cookie on a rack and pushed through the swinging kitchen door. A few people she didn't know but recognized as B&B guests stood in line at the buffet table. Most of the seating at the table was full.

Zoe caught her eye. "Feel free to sit anyplace you'd like. We're all spread out."

Maybe she'd grab a plate and head to her room. Something amazing had happened while she was decorating cookies, and she needed time alone to process.

"I believe I saw Derrick and Alyssa head outside," Zoe said.

"Okay. Thanks." Would it be rude to sequester herself in her room? Probably. She could think later. She grabbed a white ceramic plate from a small stack and filled half her plate with a green salad and the other half with a couple slices of ham then made her way to the front porch.

The Trainor clan occupied the lone table with three seats remaining. Alyssa spotted her. "Come sit with us, Hope."

She settled beside Alyssa. Derrick sat on the end and Jill sat across from them. "Wasn't that spread something?"

"Yet all you took was ham and rabbit food." Derrick sliced through a piece of ham.

She shrugged. "I happen to enjoy rabbit food." She stabbed a tomato and popped it into her mouth. The juices exploded into delicious goodness.

A man she didn't recognize walked outside holding a plate and glass. He looked around until his gaze landed on Jill. He walked in their direction, and said, "Mind if I join you?" He set his plate beside Jill and then sat. "I'm Nate." He announced to those at the table.

Jill's cheeks turned the color of the strawberries on her plate. "I'm glad you could make it. I didn't see you come in. I don't know how we missed each other."

"You were busy serving hors d'oeuvres when I arrived, and then I spotted Nick. We ended up hiding Easter eggs in the backyard."

"Thanks for helping."

"Sure. Anything for you." He winked.

Jill tucked her chin.

Derrick raised a brow. "The two of you know each other?"

Jill nodded. "We met at the church several weeks ago." She tilted her head shyly toward Nate. "We've been dating."

Derrick's eyes widened. "How did I not know this?"

Jill shrugged. "You've been in your own world."

Hope tried to look at the man without being obvious. His brown hair was neatly trimmed, and he wore khakis with a long sleeve lavender shirt. He had a boy-next-door look to him, which Jill and her niece clearly liked—

must be a family thing. Jill's bright color had faded some, but still shone a pretty shade of pink.

Good for her. She'd wondered why Derrick's sister was still single. It wasn't like she was unattractive. In fact most people would consider her pretty with her long, dark hair and classic features. Plus she had a huge heart once you got to know her.

"I'm Derrick, Jill's brother. This is my daughter Alyssa. And that is our friend Hope. How'd the two of you meet?"

"We're in the same small group at church," Nate said.

Hope hadn't realized the church had small groups. She'd love to join one, but what was the point if she was leaving the island. Her job at the resort would be finished in another week. Which begged the question—where would she live?

She needed to figure out her housing and fast. Staying on Wildflower appealed. Her feelings about Derrick were mixed, but she wanted to see where things went. Leaving the island at this point would hamper any hope they might have for a future together. She wasn't good at the long distance thing, even if it was only an hour each way.

Could she trust him with her heart? He would never hurt her on purpose. Of that she was certain, but deliberate or not, hurt was painful and she couldn't take any more pain from the people she loved.

Loved? She shot a glance in his direction. His eyes crinkled at the corners as he smiled. Yes, she'd fallen for

Derrick, and in spite of everything, she still loved him. What was she going to do? Maybe she *should* get serious about staying on the island at least for a while, and see how things went.

Jill mentioned that Rachel and her husband had a rental. Maybe it would be wise to speak with them today to see if her idea was feasible.

If the price was right, staying on the island while her house was being built would be nice. Sure, she'd have to commute to the mainland every day and would need to calculate the expense of that into the cost of living here, but the perks of staying were too good to pass up without at least checking into it.

She quickly finished her meal. "Excuse me. I need to talk with someone." She pushed back from the table and stood.

The B&B door opened, and a little boy darted out and raced around to the backyard. Was it time for the Easter egg hunt already?

Rachel and her husband, Chris, came out next. "Did anyone see a boy about this tall?" She held her hand at her waist level.

"He ran to the backyard," Hope said. "Are you leaving? I was hoping to talk with you about your rental unit. Jill mentioned it might be vacant."

Rachel glanced at her husband. "I'll find Jason while you talk with Hope."

Chris nodded. "We can talk in the sitting room. No one's in there."

Hope followed then sat in an armchair.

He took a seat on the couch. "How long are you looking to rent?"

"If the price is right I could sign a six month lease. My home caught fire and was destroyed. It hasn't even been demoed. I'll need a place to stay for at least six months to a year, possibly longer depending on how slow things move along."

He quoted the monthly price which was almost equivalent to her monthly mortgage. It'd be tough to manage both, but it wasn't like she had any other bills since the utilities were included. Maybe she'd be better off staying on at the B&B. The meals, other than breakfast, would stop as soon as her job was finished at the resort, so that could prove to be a huge inconvenience.

"Is there anyone else interested in your rental at this time?"

He shook his head. "The tenant moved out last week, and we are in the process of doing needed repairs. You're welcome to drop by anytime to check the place out. I work from home, so I'm usually there."

"Okay. If I decide I'm interested, I'll do that."

He pulled a business card from his wallet and wrote on the back. "That's the address."

"All right, then. Thanks." She shook his hand.

Derrick stepped into the room. "Hope. We need to talk."

Hope's heart rate kicked into double time. From the look on his face, she suspected whatever he had to say would be life altering.

CHAPTER FOURTEEN

DERRICK WAITED IN THE ENTRYWAY TO the B&B's sitting room, trying to be patient while Hope wrapped up her conversation with Chris.

She glanced his way. Her brow furrowed and she sucked in her bottom lip. He hadn't meant to cause her alarm, but he needed to speak with her before she did anything rash, like sign a lease on the rental at Chris and Rachel's. He didn't like the idea of her locked into anything long term. What if she hated their place after being there for a short time and was stuck in a lease? Chris nodded as he walked by him. Hope stood still as if frozen in place.

"Let's talk outside. They're about to do the Easter egg hunt for the kids. We could watch that and talk."

"Oh. Okay. What did you want to talk about?"

He almost chuckled at the strangled sound of her voice. As tough as she looked and acted, one would never know that she had such a soft, vulnerable side too. "Don't worry, Hope. It's nothing bad."

Her stance instantly relaxed. "Your tone unnerved

me and had me worried. So everything is okay?"

"Yes. I only want to run an idea by you." He gently gripped her elbow and guided her outside to where most of the guests were gathered. "I heard you talking to Chris about leasing his rental."

She nodded. "I'm not sure what I'm going to do. I think while my house is being rebuilt I'd like to stay on the island and see how things go."

How things go? Could she be saying what he thought she was? "I like the sound of that. Does that mean you're willing to pick up where we left off?"

"I'd like that very much, but I'm not ready to go there yet. Something happened to me today, and I need to spend some time with the Lord figuring things out."

"Okay. I'll give you all the space you need."

"Thanks. What did you want to talk about?"

"Your living situation."

They stopped along the edge of the area set aside for the Easter egg hunt. Spring bulbs in yellow, red, orange, and various shades of purple filled the flowerbeds making this truly feel like Easter.

Children varying in age from toddlers to ten-years-old waited to be told they could begin the hunt. He spotted his sister talking with the kids. The hunt was her brainchild, so she was responsible to make sure it went off without a hitch.

"I was going to caution you against signing a long lease agreement. I thought you might like to keep your options open." And if things progressed the way he hoped, she wouldn't need to lease. She'd be living with him as his wife. "I also was going to offer a room at my house as a last resort, but that's probably not a good idea."

She rested a hand on his forearm. "You're very sweet, Derrick. I agree with you. That would not be a good idea."

Nick sauntered their direction and stopped beside Hope. "I heard you spoke with Chris about leasing."

"News travels fast." Hope's brow scrunched.

"Chris is a good friend. I spoke with Zoe, and I believe we can help."

They listened as he quoted a price for a room at the B&B that included breakfast and a sack lunch like she'd been getting.

"I realize it's not the same as having a home with your own space, but as I understand, you are without furniture, and considering you'll be out on jobs most of the time anyway, this would save you a little money, and you wouldn't have the responsibility of cleaning."

"You and Zoe have given me a lot to think about. Thank you for your generous offer. I'll let you know my decision in the morning."

"Good." He started to walk away then stopped. "I forgot, I'm on call at the hospital tomorrow. If I miss you, please inform Jill of your decision."

"Will do."

Unsure what to say about this turn of events, Derrick stayed quiet. He'd been so afraid she'd return to the mainland and disappear from their lives.

"Did you put Nick up to that? Hope asked.

"Nope. But I can see why you'd ask." He rubbed his chin. "Whatever you decide, know that you are welcome to come to dinner at my house whenever you are able. Alyssa would love it, and so would I."

"I'll keep that in mind." She nodded once. "Today has been a little overwhelming. I really need time alone to think." She grasped his hand and gave it a light squeeze. "I'm going to my room. Please tell Jill and Alyssa goodbye for me." She rushed away.

Disappointment hit him. He'd hoped to spend more time with her today, but clearly she had a lot on her mind.

Jill shouted. "On your mark. Get set. Go!"

The kids taking part in the egg hunt scurried around the yard, each holding a cloth sack. A little girl pulled an egg out of a watering can, while Jason, Rachel and Chris's son, snatched one from inside an old metal wheelbarrow.

There was laughter and smiles all around as parents and friends watched the children. He remembered how fun Easter had been with Alyssa when she'd been little, but she'd outgrown the entertainment several years ago.

He spotted Alyssa across the yard with Jill and Nate. The guy seemed nice, and clearly his sister was smitten with him. He'd never seen her blush like she had when he'd come to sit with them. He chuckled softly at the memory.

It was about time she found someone who could make her blush. Jill had been alone for a very long time, and although she never complained, he knew she desired a family of her own.

He glanced up and spotted Hope standing at her bedroom window, looking out. Her focus went beyond the yard, probably to the Sound. It was mesmerizing even to him, and he'd been living on the island for several years.

The fact that she'd decided to stay on Wildflower while her house was being built was the first sign of encouragement he'd gotten from her that they might have a future together. He only hoped she wouldn't change her mind.

Four days later, Hope strode out the door of the final resort cabin with satisfaction. They'd finished the job a day early. She'd done little but work this past week to make the deadline. She'd sent her crew home a while ago. They'd begin a new job tomorrow in Tacoma. Everything was falling into place. She'd finally made an official decision. She was staying on the island.

Derrick had been surprisingly absent since Easter, and she was growing concerned. He'd promised her space, but she hadn't expected him to vanish from her life completely. Had he decided she wasn't worth the effort? She couldn't blame him if he had. She hadn't been overly encouraging. She glanced at her watch and sighed. He should have been here five minutes ago.

Her cell chimed, indicating a text.

Running late. Will be there soon.

Per her contract, she couldn't leave until he signed off on the work. At least she didn't have too far to go. She was now officially a resident at Wildflower Bed-and-Breakfast. Knowing the island was home made her more at ease. She'd keep an eye out for the perfect home to settle into, but for now the B&B was her new home. She would commute to the mainland as needed, but she had a trusted employee who could handle most jobs on the mainland.

This was no longer a temporary stop in her life. She could put down roots and get involved with the church and community here. Excitement bubbled inside her.

A cool breeze made her shiver. She strode to her SUV and slipped into her favorite hoodie and sat inside with the door open. The hoodie had seen better days, but its softness couldn't be beat. She loved it.

A truck approached. *Finally.* She got out and waved as Derrick pulled up beside her. She grabbed the clipboard that held the contract along with a pen for him to sign off.

He slid out. "Sorry about being late. We had several guests wanting to check in at the same time, and things got a little harried for a while." He walked toward the cabins.

She strolled beside him. "No problem. It's not like I have to catch the ferry or anything."

He stopped. "Does this mean what I think it does?"

"If you think it means that I'm staying on the island, then yes." She grinned as his eyes widened and a twinkle lit them.

"That's the best news I've had all week."

"I'm surprised you didn't know. I told Jill on Monday."

"My sister is not permitted to discuss B&B business with me."

She shrugged. "I suppose that's good. Considering everyone seems to know everyone's business around here. At least some things should be private."

He pushed into the cabin. "Good point."

She waited by the door and let him do his thing. It's funny how she no longer minded him looking over her work. Granted, it had always been her policy to have a client sign off on the job when it was finished.

She'd changed since coming to Wildflower. More than anyone yet knew.

Derrick turned and headed in her direction. "It all looks great."

"Thanks." She stepped outside and waited for him to lock up. "I need a favor."

"What's that?"

"I want to surprise Piper with the sign she asked me for, but I have nowhere to make it. Would it be possible for me to work at your place?"

A smile broke across his face. "Absolutely. When will you start?"

"I have a job in Tacoma tomorrow. While I'm there, I'll pick up the supplies and my tools from the friend who's been borrowing them. Maybe I could come by your place on Saturday."

"Sounds like a plan." He studied her eyes. "What's changed?"

She looked away, unnerved by his open curiosity. "Me."

"I can see that. I meant specifically."

"Remember when I was decorating the cookies at the B&B on Easter?"

He nodded. "I could tell something special was taking place."

"It was, but it had begun earlier in the day. I was so afraid of being hurt that it was stifling. I finally let go of the fear and then the hurt. Later that evening, I realized the weight of hurt I'd been carrying around had lifted." She shivered and tucked her hands into the pockets of her hoodie.

"So your creative juices are flowing again?"

"Yes." She grinned.

He did a fist pump. "That is great news." He wrapped her in his arms.

His body heat warmed her as she snuggled closer. "I could stand like this all day."

A laugh rumbled in his chest. "All day might be pushing it."

She leaned her head back and grinned. "Fine." She let go and stepped away, immediately missing the feel of his arms.

"Do you have dinner plans?"

She shook her head.

"Alyssa is cooking tonight. You're welcome to come."

"Will there be enough?"

"I'm sure of it. Alyssa always cooks too much. Gabe, Jill and Nate will be there too. I'd love it if you joined us."

"Sure. That sounds like fun." Although she'd prefer a romantic meal with only the two of them. "So Gabe and Alyssa are still an item, huh?"

"Yeah." He rolled his eyes. "But the big news is Nate and my sister. I was beginning to wonder if she'd ever find someone."

She playfully punched his shoulder. "That wasn't nice."

"I didn't mean it in a bad way. She's been alone for a very long time. Her last boyfriend took off when she was still in college. She hasn't so much as had one date since then."

"You're kidding. Maybe she's dated and didn't tell you."

"I suppose that's possible, but not likely. Although she didn't tell me about Nate until they'd been going out for a few weeks."

"Exactly." She looked toward her vehicle. "I should go so I can get cleaned up. What time is dinner?"

"Six."

"Okay. I'll be there."

"Good."

She couldn't wait for tonight. She had more news to tell him.

Derrick rushed through his house in a frenzy to make sure everything was perfect, including the table where he'd placed flowers. This was his second chance with Hope, and he didn't want to blow it.

He'd purchased the bouquet from the lady who'd set up shop on a street corner downtown. She specialized in wildflowers, go figure, but she still had a small selection of daffodils. He'd chosen the daffodils since he'd given Hope tulips last time.

"Relax, Dad. Gabe's coming over too, and you don't see me acting all stressed out."

He paused. "You're right, sweetie, but this is different. You've already won Gabe's heart. The verdict is still out on how Hope feels about me."

His daughter giggled. "I thought it was obvious she's crazy about you." She shrugged. "But, whatever."

She is? He wanted to ask how Alyssa knew, but discussing his love life with his teenaged daughter was a bad idea. "When will Aunt Jill be here?"

"She's riding over with Nate. I like him."

"Nate?"

"Yeah. He's really nice to Aunt Jill, and when he looks at her, his eyes get all dreamy like yours do when you look at Hope."

He squared his shoulders. "I don't get dreamy-eyed."

She rolled her eyes. "Whatever, Dad. Hey—will you keep an eye on the chicken stew while I check on the bread? I should have used a larger pot, and I'm afraid it will overflow if we aren't careful."

"Sure. You made homemade bread?"

She slid her hand into an oven glove. "Yeah. I'm surprised you don't smell it. The entire house is scented with it."

He breathed in deeply. "I smell it now. I've been going so fast since I got home I didn't take the time to notice. It smells delicious. How'd you have time? Doesn't bread need to rise and stuff?"

"Wow. You really are self-absorbed sometimes. Or maybe your thoughts are Hope-absorbed," she scrunched her nose. "That sounded funny." She shrugged. "Today was a half-day at school. I've been home since noon."

"Right. I forgot. And I'm not self-absorbed, just super busy."

"When is Piper's baby due? I'm looking forward to having my dad back."

He draped an arm across her shoulder and gave her a squeeze. "I'm sorry it's been so nuts this past month, but her baby isn't due until June."

Alyssa's head drooped. "Oh."

"Come on, kiddo. It's not that bad. All the electrical work is finished, so I won't be working so much. Besides, I'm here now. Let's make the most of it. What's for dessert?"

"Aunt Jill is bringing it."

His mouth watered. Jill had a knack for desserts. "Any idea what it is?"

"Tiramisu, I think."

"Fancy. She must really like Nate."

The doorbell rang. "I need to get that."

"Okay." She placed the golden brown bread on a cooling rack.

Before he even left the room, Gabe, Nate and Jill walked into the kitchen. "Oh, it's just you."

Jill laughed. "Thanks a lot!"

"He's nervous about Hope." Alyssa pulled open the fridge. "What does everyone want to drink?" She frowned. "Dad, you didn't stop at the general store like I asked, did you?"

His face heated. That was the reason he'd stopped downtown, but he had gotten distracted when he spotted the flower lady. "I'm sorry." He turned to face Jill and Nate. "I was on beverage duty and forgot."

Jill only smiled.

"Water's fine with me," Nate said. "You have a nice place, Derrick."

"Thanks."

"As soon as Hope gets here, we can eat." Alyssa flicked off the stove.

His cell rang. He checked the caller ID. "Everything okay, Hope?"

"No. I'm afraid not. At the last minute I had to run to the mainland to meet with my architect, and I missed the ferry. I will get there as soon as I can."

Disappointment washed through him. She'd be at least another hour.

CHAPTER FIFTEEN

Hope pulled up to Derrick's house and rushed to the door. She was so late. The ferry had a problem that needed to be fixed before it could take another run. She should have been here an hour ago. To make matters worse, her cell phone battery died right after she called Derrick to let him know she'd missed the ferry, so she couldn't call back and let him know to expect her even later. She raised her hand to knock, but it swung open before she could.

"You made it!" Alyssa hugged her. "My dad is a nervous wreck. When you didn't show up and he couldn't reach you on your cell . . ." She shuddered. "Go easy on him." She turned to walk away.

"Wait!" Hope said in a stage whisper. "Why is he nervous?"

She looked over her shoulder presumably to where Derrick waited. "You know my mom died in a car accident, right?"

Hope nodded.

"Well, she was rushing home from an appointment

on the mainland. She took a corner too fast and lost control. I think maybe—"

"No need to say more. I understand." She followed Alyssa into the family room.

Jill jumped up from her seat on the sofa, rushed to Hope, and pulled her into a hug. "I'm so glad you made it. We were worried. You should've called."

"My phone died." She had no idea how upset they would be or she'd have borrowed someone's phone and had Piper call, since that was the only number she had memorized.

"Is Dad still in his office?"

Jill nodded. "You better get in there, Hope, before he has a meltdown."

"I'm so sorry to upset all of you." She looked past Jill to Nate. "I hope you at least ate dessert."

Nate shook his head. "It's good to see you again."

Jill pushed her toward the hall. "Hurry."

Hope's heart pounded. This was not how she'd expected tonight to go. She knocked softly on his office door. "Derrick. It's Hope."

The door yanked open. He pulled her in his arms. "I was so worried." His heart pounded against her ear.

"I know. I'm sorry." She explained what happened.

He finally released her. "You need a portable charger. I'm buying you one tomorrow."

"Thanks, but I can take care of it. Are you going to be okay?"

"Yes. I'm sorry for overreacting."

"I understand. Alyssa told me about your wife."

His lips pressed together in a frown.

To see him so torn up, she realized exactly how much he cared about her, and she was doubly glad she'd decided to stay on the island. But if they were going to have a relationship, one thing needed to change. She took his hand and drew him over to a loveseat beside his desk. "Have you ever prayed about your fear?"

He turned startled eyes toward her. "This has never happened before."

"But I guarantee it *will* happen again. Alyssa is getting her driver's license soon, and if you are anything like my dad, you will worry every time she gets behind the wheel of a car."

"I thought your dad was a cop."

"Exactly. He's seen too much."

"Oh."

"Not too long ago, after I met you and Alyssa, I asked him how he handled having a teenage driver." She chuckled. "He admitted he had his fellow officers keep an eye out for me, and if there was a problem they were to call him. Thankfully, he never received a call."

"But my dad wasn't a Christian at that time, as you are. You can ask the Lord to help you. He will take that fear away if you let Him."

Derrick settled deeper into the loveseat in his office and

swallowed the lump that had formed in his throat. "I did pray, but I couldn't stop worrying."

He took Hope's hand and placed a kiss on her palm. "What you're suggesting is easier said than done, but thank you for that reminder. I'll try to do better next time." Should there be a next time. He sincerely hoped there wouldn't. In the meantime, he planned to enjoy every second he could with this woman who had captured his heart. "Let's get you some food."

"Oh, good. I was hoping you'd remember. I'm starving." She bounded off the couch, dragging him along with her.

He chuckled. "Remind me to never get between you and food."

"Ha-ha. It so happens lunch was eight hours ago."

"Then why are you in here with me? You should have gone straight to the kitchen." He pulled her forward and into the kitchen. "I hope you like chicken stew."

"Even if I didn't, I'd eat it."

He ladled a generous serving from the pot that had been left to simmer on the stove. "Would you like homemade bread? For a beginner, I think Alyssa did a great job on it."

"Sure." Hope took the bowl and the sliced bread he handed her to the table and sat. "This smells delicious."

"Thanks!" Alyssa walked into the room and sat across from her. "Do you mind if we have dessert while you eat?"

"Not at all."

Hand-in-hand, Jill and Nate meandered into the

room. It looked like his sister and Nate had fallen hard for one another. He preferred to take things slow, but he wouldn't mind a little more handholding himself. His fear dissipated and left in its place an acute awareness that he wanted Hope to be a part of his life for a very long time.

Hope and Alyssa giggled over something.

"What'd I miss?"

Hope tilted her head toward his sister and Nate who were clearly lost in themselves.

"Where's Gabe?" He'd just realized the teen was missing.

"He needed to go home," Alyssa said. "Aunt Jill, the tiramisu is yummy. Will you teach me to make it?"

"Sure, sweetie." Jill's focus never left Nate.

Derrick pretended to gag himself.

Hope chuckled. "Behave yourself. I'm sure you've felt the same way at some point."

"Sure, but I don't act like a love-struck teenager."

"That's what you think," Alyssa said, rolling her eyes.

He shot her a warning look.

His daughter raised her hands. "Sorry." She stood and rinsed her dish. "I'm going to my room."

"So early?" Hope asked.

"It's been a super long day, and I'm tired. Goodnight, everyone."

Hope looked at him with questioning eyes. "Is that normal?"

"My daughter has never been a night owl." He was glad too, since it made it easier to get her to school on time.

Hope leaned back in the chair and patted her stomach. "I'm stuffed. Think I'll pass on dessert."

If he had to sit in the room much longer with the lovebirds, he might lose his dinner. "Want to take a walk?"

"It's dark out"

"Don't worry. I'll protect you from the bats."

Her face paled. "There are bats here too?"

"I was only teasing. I have never seen a bat flying around my home." He'd never forget her priceless reaction to the little brown bat they'd encountered at the B&B.

"In that case. A walk sounds nice. Besides, I have something to tell you."

Curiosity piqued, he stood and cleared the dishes. "You ready?"

"Yep."

He reached for her hand, his heart racing. Okay, so maybe he was a little love-struck too.

CHAPTER SIXTEEN

Glad for the cover of darkness, Hope gave Derrick's hand a light squeeze before pulling hers from his grasp and tucking her hands into her pockets. Her brain turned to mush when he held her hand, and she needed to think clearly.

"I have something to tell you." It's funny how earlier today she couldn't wait to share her news, but now uncertainty gripped her.

"So you've said. Is something wrong?" Concern edged Derrick's voice.

She took a deep breath and let it out slowly. "The thing is, I like Wildflower Island, and I've grown very fond of the people here." She licked her lips. "I realized something else on Easter that I didn't mention earlier today."

"What was that?" he asked softly.

Why was this so hard to say? "The Lord showed me that He can create beauty anywhere—including in my wounded heart. I've been so afraid of being hurt again that I've wrapped myself in a cocoon. You broke through that cocoon and made me see what I'm missing."

He slid an arm across her shoulder and snuggled her close. "I'm very happy to hear that. But I'm really curious what happened on Easter to open your eyes. Whatever it was must have been momentous."

She wrapped both arms around him in a side hug and rested her cheek against the side of his chest. "I only told you part of what happened while I was decorating the cookies. God showed me that He can take something that appears plain and void of anything nice and make it beautiful. That's how my heart felt after my mother did what she did. I felt a void inside me—unable to feel anything. I shut down. But now, everything is different. I feel alive again, and my brain won't shut off. I have so many ideas for sculptures."

He kissed the top of her head. "I'm so happy for you. If there is anything you need, let me know."

"You've been a huge help already by agreeing to allow me to work here. I can't wait to surprise Piper with a sign for the boathouse."

"You mentioned growing fond of the people here. Does that mean you're going to stay on permanently?"

"I hope to. I'm going to sell the lot, or put my house in Tacoma on the market as soon as possible. I'm still thinking through my decision."

Two weeks later, Hope enlisted Derrick to hang the new

sign on the boathouse. Sunshine glinted off the bronze colored metal sculpture. She'd spent last weekend making it but had been too busy working off the island to get it over to the resort. She was more than pleased with the end result. The playful sculpture with a stork inside a canoe would forever remind her of Piper. Hopefully Piper would love it.

Derrick stood by her side with an arm draped across her shoulder. "You should send a picture to Piper."

"I did. She hasn't replied."

"That's because I had to see it in person." Piper ambled toward them.

Hope rushed to her friend's side. "What are you doing here?"

"I wanted to see it for myself. This is history in the making." Piper's face glowed as she peered at the art above the door. "It's some of your best work. Thank you for doing this for me. I know how difficult it was for you."

Hope's face heated. "You're welcome and thanks for asking me to do it. I hated to say no to you. Your request forced me to make a big change in my life."

Piper raised a brow. "It's different than your other work. Still whimsical, but it has more depth. I love it." She faced Hope. "Seeing this is worth risking the wrath of Chase when he hears I came here."

"You think so, huh?" Chase approached wearing a loving smile.

Piper planted her hands where her waist should be and let out a breath of exasperation. "How'd you know where to find me?"

"I have spies all over the island." He waggled his brows then kissed her and held her close. "Actually I was already here working in one of the plant beds when I saw you."

Hope chuckled and moved to Derrick's side. She lowered her voice. "I think this is our cue to leave."

"Good idea," he whispered back. "I see an open paddle boat. Shall we?"

Her stomach leaped. "I've always wanted to do that! See you love birds later."

Derrick grasped her hand. "Let's get moving." They went into the boat barn. He sorted things out with the guy manning the counter while she looked at souvenirs. A minute later Derrick sauntered over to her. "You ready?"

"Yep. Looks like Chase already whisked Piper home. I can't believe she drove over here."

"Then you don't know her like I thought you did."

"Good point. That act of rebellion was classic Piper. Exactly like her showing up at the B&B on Easter. But I know she would never do anything to harm her baby. Her blood pressure must have improved."

"Either that or she was going stir crazy and figured a little jaunt over here wasn't a big deal. She lives close enough she could have walked."

"True." She motioned toward the boat. "You still want to do this?"

"Are you kidding? I've been hoping to ride in one of these since I started working here but never had a good excuse." He kissed her forehead. "Thanks."

"My pleasure." She stepped into the boat then rested her feet on the pedals and waited for Derrick to get settled.

"Here we go."

Together they pedaled away from the shore. A few other boaters were in the water but steered clear of them. They made their way to the middle of the lake and stopped.

Hope took in the sites around her. Fir trees surrounded three sides of the lake. The resort took up one side, and the architecture fit so nicely with the rustic surroundings. Piper was an amazing architect in her own right. If her friend weren't on bed rest, she'd have hired her to draw up the design for her house rather than Duncan. Then again, Piper would have enjoyed it, but what was done was done. "It's pretty out here."

"Mmm-hmm."

She shifted to better face him and noticed his gaze focused on her. "What?" She smiled.

He shrugged. "I'm happy."

"Me too." She couldn't imagine any place she'd rather be or anyone else she'd rather be with than Derrick. "I could do this every weekend and it would never grow old." That is, *as long as I'm with him.*

"I don't know if I'd go that far." He chuckled. "But I *would* enjoy the company."

She glanced his way. "I was thinking the same thing. I have to admit, when Piper first told me that we would be perfect for each other, I blamed it on her pregnancy hormones."

"And now?"

"Now, I'd say she knew exactly what she was talking about." She watched a group of kids along the shoreline playing tag. "You want to hear the irony of it all?" She didn't wait for his reply. "I didn't think you were my type based on how you dressed. Me, the woman who is constantly pre-judged by people because of my tattoos, did the exact same thing to you."

"A wise person once told me not to judge a book by its cover."

"That wise woman wouldn't happen to be Piper?" She'd heard her friend say that many times through the years. It was a favorite mantra.

He nodded. "I'm glad I listened."

"Me too."

He leaned toward her and softly kissed her lips. "I want to ask you something."

"Sure."

"How do you feel about long courtships?"

She almost laughed at the old fashioned word, but stopped herself in time when she saw the sincerity in his eyes. "I think they're overrated."

"Me too." He slid his hand into his jeans' pocket and pulled something out. "I know we haven't known each other long, but when it's right, you know." He held out a princess cut diamond ring set in white gold.

She caught her breath. He was proposing! It was true they hadn't known each other long, but in her heart, she knew he was the man for her, even if he was a dad. "What about Alyssa? Did you—"

"Thank you for caring what my daughter thinks. That is one more reason I love you, and for the record, she gave her blessing."

Hope's face hurt from smiling.

"Will you marry me?"

"Absolutely!"

He slid the beautiful ring onto her finger. "Perfect." He raised an arm in the air in a fist pump.

Screaming broke out from the shore. Hope's gaze darted that way. She narrowed her eyes. "Is that Alyssa and Jill?"

He nodded. "They knew I was proposing today."

"But how? The boat was a spur of the moment idea."

"Not really. I'd already reserved it, and it was waiting for us. I've had this planned for several days."

She playfully punched him in the arm. "It looks like surprising people runs in the family." They paddled back to the dock and tied up.

Alyssa ran toward them and barreled into them. "I'm so glad you said yes. He's been nervous all week."

Jill strolled toward them wearing a huge smile. "Congratulations!" She hugged each of them. "I have some news of my own." She held out her left hand. "Nate proposed last night."

Moving fast must be another family trait. "Congratulations to you too," Hope said.

Derrick looked dumbstruck. "Yeah. Wow. Who would have thought we'd both get engaged so close together?"

Hope looked at the group that would be her new

family and her insides warmed. When she came to this island she never dreamed she'd find the man of her dreams, much less get her passion for art back. This was definitely an island filled with hope.

Derrick tugged her close. "I forgot something." He lowered his mouth to hers sealing their engagement with a kiss.

EPILOGUE

October

"I CAN'T BELIEVE IT'S MY WEDDING day." Hope caught Jill's eye in the mirror in one of the Sunday school rooms that had been converted to a dressing room. She reached up and stuck a decorative pin in her hair.

Jill stood to her right adjusting her veil with a pretty beaded edge. "*Our* wedding day." She ran her hands down her white strapless wedding dress.

Hope nodded in agreement. Some would say they were rushing it, but when the timing was right, it was right. When Jill had come to her with the idea of a double wedding, she couldn't pass it up. How special to have brother and sister married in the same ceremony?

A light tap on the door drew her attention. "Want me to get it?"

Jill shook her head. "Who is it?"

"Nate and Derrick," Derrick said. "May we come in and pray with you ladies?"

Jill's face lit, and she shot Hope a panicked look.

"You can't see us before the wedding."

Hope's heart melted that they would think of this. No way would she turn them away. "Hold on a second, guys."

Jill grasped her arm. "What are you doing?"

"Trust me." Hope sashayed to the door and opened it barely enough that they could hear one another easily, but no one would be able to see in. "Okay. Go ahead and pray." She heard chuckling from the other side of the door.

"Lord," Derrick said. "We thank You for these ladies and what a blessing they are to us. We ask that You will bless our marriages and that You will be the center of our relationships. Amen."

Nate prayed next.

They all said amen together.

Jill dabbed a tear from her eye. "That was beautiful. Thank you. Now go away so we can finish getting ready."

Hope giggled like a schoolgirl as happiness bubbled up. "I'm so glad we decided to keep things simple."

Jill nodded. "That dress is perfect on you too."

"Thanks." Hope stood before a full-length mirror and admired the vintage three-quarter length, sleeved dress she'd found at a boutique here on the island. She'd looked everywhere she could for a solid month trying to find one that covered her Captain Jack tattoo. She had found a couple, but they didn't wow her. On a whim, she'd stopped at the boutique and discovered this little gem. The full skirt and midi length of the dress reminded her of something Audrey Hepburn might have worn.

Jill applied a coat of red lipstick then pressed her lips together. "Won't this color red look good on Nate?"

Hope laughed. "You are bad." Her phone alarm went off, indicating it was time to go. She pressed the alarm button, silencing it. "Shall we?"

Jill's eyes twinkled as she smiled. She looped an arm through Hope's, and together they left the room. Their dads each met them at the entrance to the sanctuary. Someone pulled open the door leading down the center aisle, which had a white runner leading to the front where their grooms, and other members of the wedding party, waited.

Hope and Jill had both agreed that Zoe, Piper, and Alyssa should be their attendants. The three girls wore lacy purple sheath dresses that stopped right above their knees. The stage had a large, single arrangement of multicolored wildflowers.

A string quartet played Pachelbel's Cannon in D as Hope walked arm in arm with her father down the aisle, then Jill followed with her dad.

The ceremony went fast, and before Hope knew it she was Mrs. Derrick Trainor and a step-mother! Now there was something she'd never believed she'd be. Alyssa hugged them both and promised to meet up with them at the B&B where the reception would take place.

Derrick guided her up the aisle and into her dressing room, then pulled her close. "I wish we could skip the reception and go straight to the honeymoon."

"That would be nice, but then we'd miss the cake, and I want cake."

He laughed. "Whatever you want, my love."

She wrapped her arms around his neck as he lowered his mouth to hers and gave her a toe-curling kiss. "I want more of that. Much more."

A Sneak Peek at an Upcoming New Series

A Love to Treasure
Sunriver Dreams: Book One

By: Kimberly Rose Johnson

Chapter One

NICOLE DAVIS DROVE PAST A HUGE welcome sign to Sunriver, Oregon, and grinned. She was finally here. She loved this resort community and still couldn't believe it would be home for the next few months.

She bore to the right around the one-way traffic circle. A black car came out of nowhere. Nicole swerved and slammed on the brake, her front bumper barely missing the side of the black car. Her heart pounded as she weaved her Mini Cooper onto the miniscule dirt shoulder a few feet from a large pine tree. She put the car in park. She looked around to make sure she hadn't hit anything. *Whew.* Everything looked okay.

The crazy driver who ran her off the road drove around the circle again and pulled off the road in front of her. This couldn't be good. She gulped as a man with thick dark hair, wearing jeans and a dark gray T-shirt moved from the black car and stalked toward her.

Her stomach clenched. She checked her reflection in the rearview mirror and noted her wide green eyes filled with fear. *Not good.* She needed to at least appear unaffected by the incident or he'd think her vulnerable. She took a deep breath then let it out in a quick puff. After making sure no cars were coming, she stepped out of her Mini Cooper and onto the shoulder, refusing to be intimidated by the handsome man. His height caught her by surprise. Most men were only a few inches taller than her, but not this guy. He towered above her five-foot-nine-inch frame—and those biceps. Maybe she should've stayed in the car, he could crush her. Then again, he didn't look dangerous, only irritated.

She offered him a tentative smile. "That was a close call."

"No kidding. You didn't yield." He pointed to a yellow sign.

"Oops. Sorry." Her face heated. Grams always said she barreled through life. But, she generally obeyed the traffic signs. "I didn't see the sign."

She focused on the handsome man before her with dark brown eyes the color of Swiss chocolate.

His brows scrunched down. "Are you okay?"

Her gaze dropped to his mouth, pulled into a frown. She shook her head and focused on the concern in his eyes. "I'm fine. No harm done as they say. And I really am sorry about not yielding." She backed against the car door. Her grandmother had paid for this adventure, and she *would* enjoy it—she just needed to be more careful. "I haven't been to Sunriver in years and was trying to find the resort lodge." She took in her surroundings—a paved bicycle trail, roadway, and woods. Beyond the woods she spotted several structures dotting the landscape. "I don't suppose you could point me in the right direction."

He peered down at her, his stance relaxing. He even ventured what appeared to be a small smile. "Like you said, no harm done." He pointed slightly left. "The lodge is that way."

The breeze rustling through the tall pine trees didn't help the heat burning in Nicole's cheeks. "Thanks."

"No problem. Watch for the signs. They'll keep you on track." He sauntered back to his car, then pivoted. "By the way, welcome to Sunriver. I hope the rest of your stay goes better."

"Uh. Thanks." Nicole slid behind the wheel and drove away, hoping she wouldn't run into that man again. Talk about embarrassing! She breathed in deeply of the pine-scented air and focused on her reason for being here—Grams' letter. She owed it to her Grandmother to fulfill her final wish.

Nicole turned left into the resort lodge's parking lot and pulled into a spot. The lodge was even prettier than she remembered. The planters, a combination of red, purple and white flowers mixed among shrubs and trees, were perfection. She got out and walked toward the large entrance. The sound of crashing water drew her attention to the right. A beautiful rock water feature off of the main entrance looked like the perfect place to escape the busyness of life.

She dragged her attention away from the waterfall and climbed the concrete steps to the lodge entrance. The huge door opened with surprising ease. She pulled off her sunglasses and allowed her eyes to adjust to the dim lighting. To her left several smartly dressed people stood behind a counter waiting to check in guests.

Nicole squared her shoulders and marched toward check-in, trying to ignore the knot in the pit of her stomach. Why was she so nervous? Grams loved scavenger hunts, and this vacation promised to be an adventure, beginning with the letter that led her to the resort lodge.

Nicole approached the first person at the long reception counter. "Hi, I'm Nicole Davis. I have a reservation."

The woman smiled. "Welcome to Sunriver. I love your hair color. Is it natural?"

Nicole nodded. "Yes and thanks." Grams had loved her long blonde hair as well.

"You're lucky." She lowered her voice. "Mine's from a bottle." She sighed then clicked on the computer keyboard. She raised a brow. "You have a package. I'll be right back."

A package—*so the game begins*. Grams had a creative streak few could compete with. The package would likely contain the first clue to this adventure Grams had sent her on.

The woman came back and held out a small box wrapped in bright red paper with a shiny white bow on top.

"Thank you."

"You're welcome." She handed her a key card, then showed her where her room was on the map and explained how to get to it. "Enjoy your stay."

Nicole pocketed the key. "Thanks. I'll try." She left the building and followed the path to the stairwell that led to her suite. What was in the box? Whatever it was, she knew Grams had put a lot of thought into it.

Nicole's throat burned at the thought of her late Grandmother—so much regret. If only she'd spent more time with Grams and less time working on lesson plans this past year. She loved her grandmother and wished for a do-ever, but death didn't give do-overs. Instead, Nicole would honor her grandmother's final wish and play along one last time. Hopefully this game wouldn't end in disaster like the time when she'd ended up in the middle of a lake with a broken oar.

After changing into his uniform, Mark Stone strapped on a helmet and straddled his bicycle outside the Sunriver police department. Soon heat would rise from the pavement and make him long for the cooler paths wending their way through the tall pine trees. Hopefully his first day on the job would go better than the drive getting here. If all the tourists were like that blonde . . . oh, boy. But he had to give her credit for admitting her mistake. She seemed like a nice enough person, and she was definitely easy to look at with her long hair and emerald green eyes.

"Morning." A stocky officer strode up with his hand extended. "I'm Spencer. If you need anything let me know."

"Mark Stone. Thanks." He grasped the younger man's hand and gave it a firm shake. Spencer looked to be middle to late twenties, with sandy blond hair and piercing eyes. He reminded Mark of himself at that age—eager, and ready to take on the world, but that was then. Life had a way of changing a person.

Spencer's eyebrows narrowed. "I heard you like working alone."

Mark gave him an easy grin. Seemed the rumor mill worked overtime, if they were talking about him. "True." An image exploded in his mind knocking him back to another time and place—the reason he no longer worked with a partner. The reason he'd fled Portland, Oregon, and come to the resort town. Thankfully his superiors were more than happy to let him work alone due to budget issues.

"Guess I better get busy. Nice to meet you."

Spencer nodded then headed inside. He seemed like

someone Mark would enjoy getting to know despite his digging into a sore subject. Mark shook off the thought and pushed forward, focusing on the paved trail in front of him.

He passed a couple jogging and settled into an easy rhythm. One thing was certain; he'd be in great shape by summer's end. Cool air brushed his face. In a fenced pasture, tall grass swayed in the breeze. He could definitely get used to this. Sunriver was a far cry from the intensity of working in the big city.

He braked at a stop sign before crossing the road and went left along the path that ran past the stables. The only sound was the whir of his tires on the pavement. He caught up to three riders in no particular hurry. "On your left."

The women moved their bikes into a single file. The middle woman looked over her shoulder, wobbled, and a mere second later bumped into the leader, yelped, and the two went down. The last bike couldn't avoid the heap and joined the jumbled bodies.

Mark braked hard and jumped off. Bending over the women, he peered down and scanned for injuries. "Anyone hurt?"

Silence greeted his question. His heart hammered. He assessed each of the women quickly but couldn't see any visible injuries.

The women met each other's eyes. Then a soft snort escaped the redhead. The woman to her right erupted in a fit of giggles. In a moment the three of them were leaning against each other, laughing.

He squatted to their level. "I take it everyone is okay." He grinned and offered his hand.

"Yes, officer." The redhead brushed her palms together, then grasped his hand. "I guess I shouldn't have followed so closely."

He pulled her up before offering a hand to her friend.

A dark haired woman rolled her eyes. "Tina, you and tailgating go together like peanut butter and jelly. Come on. Let's get a move on before Connor gets too far ahead of us."

"Connor?" Mark couldn't squelch his curiosity.

The woman nodded and brushed her hands off on her denim shorts. "Yes, my thirteen-year-old cousin is visiting for the summer, and believe me, he's a handful." She pursed her lips. "Maybe I shouldn't have said that. I just meant—"

"Don't worry, I understand teenagers." Mark chuckled. "I was a handful myself at his age."

The woman gave him a grateful smile. "I'm Sarah, and these are my reckless friends, Tina and Marge."

Tina righted her bike and blatantly checked out Mark. "We're staying in Sarah's Circle Four Ranch Cabin. Would you like to join us tonight for a barbeque? It's the least we can do, considering."

The other two nodded.

"Sorry, ladies, but thanks for the offer."

Tina slipped a business card into his hand and winked. "Call me."

The women mounted their bikes and pedaled away.

Mark rubbed his neck. That was awkward, but at

least they were gone, and he dodged their dinner invitation. Nothing against assertive women, but that trio left him feeling like a piece of meat. He much preferred the blonde who ran him off the road—not that it mattered.

DISCUSSION QUESTIONS

1. When Derrick first met Hope, he appeared to judge her based on her appearance. Piper warned him against judging Hope based on her appearance. Have you ever met someone who first struck you one way, but after getting to know them, your opinion changed? Did you struggle with judging and what can you do to keep that from happening again?

2. Hope's mother hurt her a lot. Do you think Hope handled the situation well? If not, how do you think she should have dealt with her mom? Have you ever had anyone you loved betray your trust? How can you get past an experience like that and come out whole?

3. It's easy to say we need to forgive and forget when someone does us wrong. I think most people would agree that as Christians we *need* to forgive, but what about forgetting? What are your thoughts?

4. Derrick took to heart Hope's advice on how to deal with his daughter's boyfriend situation, even though he'd been hurt by busybody women after his wife died. Do you think you would have been able to take someone else's advice, or would you have tried to do it on your own?

5. Hope and Derrick at first look seemed to be an unlikely couple. What do you think it was about them that drew them to one another? Have you ever been attracted to someone who didn't seem to be a good fit? Did it work out or not, and if not, why not?

Kimberly loves connecting with her readers.

You may find her at:
http://kimberlyrjohnson.com

Facebook
https://www.facebook.com/KimberlyRoseJohnson

Twitter @kimberlyrosejoh

You may also follow her on Amazon to be notified
every time she has a new book release
by using the following link:
http://www.amazon.com/Kimberly-Rose-
Johnson/e/B00K10CR6E

BOOKS BY
KIMBERLY ROSE JOHNSON

Wildflower B&B Romance Series

Island Refuge

Island Dreams

Island Christmas

Releasing Spring 2016

Island Hope

Standalone

A Valentine for Kayla

Series with Heartsong Presents

The Christmas Promise

A Romance Rekindled

A Holiday Proposal

A Match for Meghan

www.ingramcontent.com/pod-product-compliance
Lightning Source LLC
Chambersburg PA
CBHW070949180726
48291CB00004B/1208